TAKING LIVES

A Lives Trilogy Prequel

JOSEPH LEWIS

Black Rose Writing | Texas

©2021 by Joseph Lewis
All rights reserved. No part of this book may be reproduced, stored in a retrieval system or transmitted in any form or by any means without the prior written permission of the publishers, except by a reviewer who may quote brief passages in a review to be printed in a newspaper, magazine or journal.

The author grants the final approval for this literary material.

First printing

This is a work of fiction. Names, characters, businesses, places, events, and incidents are either the products of the author's imagination or used in a fictitious manner. Any resemblance to actual persons, living or dead, or actual events is purely coincidental.

ISBN: 978-1-68433-772-9
PUBLISHED BY BLACK ROSE WRITING
www.blackrosewriting.com

Printed in the United States of America
Suggested Retail Price (SRP) $17.95

Taking Lives is printed in Garamond

*As a planet-friendly publisher, Black Rose Writing does its best to eliminate unnecessary waste to reduce paper usage and energy costs, while never compromising the reading experience. As a result, the final word count vs. page count may not meet common expectations.

Taking Lives is dedicated to all missing children. May they be found and brought home and may their families heal.

Mostly, *Taking Lives* is dedicated to Jacob Wetterling, a boy from St. Joseph, Minnesota, who was kidnapped from his hometown at the age of 11 on Sunday, October 22, 1989. His remains were given to his family after the perpetrator confessed to Jacob's abduction and murder. He is currently in prison.

TAKING LIVES

"Coyote is always out there waiting, and coyote is always hungry."
—**Navajo**

"Good and Evil are Constantly at War, and Good Men Must Choose."
—**Nelson Mandela**

CHAPTER ONE

Victorville, California
Two Years Previous . . .

Pete slipped on a pair of blue surgical gloves and knelt down on one knee next to the ME. Summer did the same, but on the other side of the body.

Because it was desert, there was some decay and a whole lot of stink, but that didn't bother Kelliher much. Not at all, actually. What bothered him was that the dead body they were examining was that of a boy, whose life was taken and extinguished way before it should have been.

"The desert air is dry, so there isn't the amount of decomposition and decay you might find, let's say, in the Midwest, but I'm guessing this kid has been here for forty-eight hours, give or take. Looking at the dark sand around the boy's head, I would say that was a blood pool, and he was shot right here, with a small caliber weapon. I'd say a .38. Entry looks to be from above and behind, so the boy was kneeling, and the shooter stood behind him. You can see stippling and some powder burns, so it was at close range. We'll get samples from the sand, but I think that's what we'll find."

"I'm guessing this boy was what, twelve or thirteen or so?" Pete asked.

The ME nodded and said, "That seems about right. Could be a little older."

"What do you make of the marks on the boy's back?" Summer asked.

The ME sighed and shook his head in disgust. "I can't be absolutely certain until I get him back to the lab, but I think he was whipped with a strap. I'd guess leather. I'll know better when I perform an autopsy."

"And the mark on his left ankle?" Pete asked. "It looks like an upside-down cross. Was that branded on him?"

"Looks that way," the ME answered quietly.

"I'm going to get a picture of the boy's face and send it to the National Center for Missing Children. Hopefully, John Clark and his team will find a match." Summer said.

"Jesus Christ," Pete said. "What are we dealing with?"

She knew what Pete was thinking, because she was thinking the same thing. Two dead boys found in the same position, in the same way, one in the High Desert of California off I-15, the route that would take one to Vegas, and the other, north of Reno and west of Gerlach, in the Smoke Creek Desert of Nevada. And just like the other boy that was found, there was no doubt in Pete's or her mind the autopsy will find signs of forced sex. The only differences between the two boys was that the fourteen-year-old boy found in Nevada, Blake from California, had dark hair, while this boy, had sandy blond hair. And Blake didn't have a brand on his ankle like this kid did.

Pete stood up, beat a little sand from his pant leg, stretched his sore back and faced the three young men, still sitting on or standing near their dirt bikes.

"Okay, which one of you discovered the body?"

Agent Pete Kelliher worked out of D.C., with the Crimes Against Children Unit, sometimes called Kiddie Cops by other agents. Before that, he had been a detective with Baltimore homicide. He and his partner, Agent Summer Storm, had flown just over two hours by plane out of Reagan National to Ontario International Airport, forty miles east of L.A., and then jumped into a helicopter and flew another twenty minutes or so up into the High Desert area east of Victorville, where this boy was found nude, handcuffed, and dead.

A long-haired, twenty-something, dark male dressed in lime-green leathers, coated in dust and dirt raised his hand. "Me. I found him."

Kelliher nodded at him. "Can you step over here, so we can talk?"

He moved off and away from lime-green's two buddies, fellow dirt bikers, and waited for lime-green to join him and Storm.

"Your name is . . ."

"Herc Moffet."

"Herc?" Summer asked.

"Hercule."

Storm pursed her lips and nodded.

"Go through your story for us, please." Summer asked tiredly.

"My friends and I come up here on Saturdays and ride. You know, just messing around. Usually, we ride on the other side of I-15, south of Hesperia, but we wanted to do something different, so we came over here on the Victorville side. We know the museum is over here, so we needed to stay away from there."

"Museum?" Pete asked.

"Yeah, the Roy Rogers Museum. It's back there about three or four miles."

Summer recalled seeing the structure from the helicopter and wondered what it was. "Okay, go on," Summer said.

"We were racing and I shot over that little ledge," he said, pointing at a rocky outcrop that looked a lot steeper than *a little ledge.*

Kelliher and Storm exchanged a look, and then turned back to Moffet.

"I damn near landed on top of him. I knew Clancy was on my tail and Devin comin' on quick, so I ran back up the ledge and flagged them down before they landed on me and the kid."

"And you guys have never biked here before?" Kelliher asked.

Moffet shook his head. "No, never, first time," he looked over his shoulder at the dead kid and added. "Shit, probably won't ever again."

Herc Moffet and his buddies, Tommy Clancy and Devin White were in their second year at Cal State San Bernardino. Moffet studied Mass Communications. Clancy was in Pre-Law, and White, Pre-Med.

Background checks on all three had been completed by a computer geek attached to Kiddie Corps, and all three were clean. Moffet worked part-time as a bartender. Clancy didn't hold any job, while White did work-study in the library.

After questioning Moffet, Kelliher and Storm turned their attention to Clancy and White, who gave virtually the same account. There didn't seem to be any inconsistency or any cause to doubt them.

Before they let them go, Summer said, "Hey guys, before you leave, do you have cell phones?"

"Yeah, sure," Moffet answered for them, while Clancy and White nodded.

"You fellas on Facebook, Twitter, and maybe Instagram?"

"Some," Clancy said warily.

Kelliher nodded and smiled knowingly.

"Just so you know," Summer said. "If any pictures appear on anything, and that would include on your device or on anyone else's device, you will be tampering with a crime scene, interfering with a criminal investigation, and any chance you have of finishing college or getting into grad school will be flushed down the toilet."

The three guys paled.

"So, what I would like you to do right now is to delete every picture you took of that little boy, and delete any post you made on any social media. You have one minute," she turned to her partner. "Pete, get ready to call Chet and let him know to begin a search of their media, because if everything isn't erased in,"

JOSEPH LEWIS 3

she made a show of looking at her watch, "forty seconds, I will arrest these gentlemen on federal charges."

Cell phones came out of pockets and fingers flew over the keys.

She waited a bit, and for good measure to prod them on, Summer said. "Twelve, eleven, ten . . ."

"Okay, okay, wait a minute." Moffet said in panic.

When she was satisfied they were done, she said. "Okay, you guys can go, but if there are any comments anywhere to anyone and we find out, same holds true about compromising our investigation."

"You can't be serious." Clancy protested.

Kelliher walked up to him. "Son, do you really think we're anything but serious?"

Clancy took a step back, looked over his shoulder at Moffet, looked back at Kelliher, and shook his head.

After the three men jumped on their bikes and rode off, Pete and Summer huddled away from the ME and his assistant, and away from the two San Bernardino Sheriff Deputies, and the two FBI agents out of LA.

"What are you thinking?"

Pete looked at her. "You already know what I think."

Summer nodded sadly.

Pete was fiftyish, had a paunch, a head of mostly gray hair on his head in a neat and tidy flattop. He looked military, but was actually quite the opposite. He might have pulled his .45 six or seven times, but he hadn't fired it in years, though he was an excellent shot. He was considered by many in the FBI as a cop's cop, a true investigator who had a good mind, who was thorough and detailed. Pete tended to be a loner who never married. He was mostly serious, mostly quiet, and off the job. He kept to himself, often watching Clint Eastwood or John Wayne movies in the dark of his living room, in his three bedroom Colonial, in Georgetown.

His partner received her first name because she was born in the backseat of a station wagon on a hot July night, with hail, thunder and lightning rocking the car. Her parents thought first of Hailey, but settled on Summer, liking how it sounded together: Summer Storm. Pete was old enough to be her father and saw her—and even treated her—as his daughter, and she grumbled about it, but Pete paid no attention. The FBI recruited her out of the University of Louisville where she had graduated from law school.

They were an odd team. Pete, sullen, rumpled and gray. Summer, trim and proper. Together, they were very good at what they did.

"We have two boys. Both nude, both handcuffed, both shot at close range in the back of the head twice with a .38. This boy was branded, while the other kid wasn't. That and hair color are the only differences. We don't know yet, but I'm willing to bet this boy here will have the same signs of forced sex that the other boy had."

Summer nodded. "We know the first boy we found, Blake Johnson. He's been missing for two years from Spokane. His parents suspected he was kidnapped."

"So, you think maybe, whoever kidnapped Blake, also took this boy?"

"And if that's the case," Summer said.

"Then we might have a serial abductor, a pedophile, preying on pre-pubescent boys," Pete answered for her.

"And if that's the case, just how many other boys are out there?" Summer wondered out loud.

CHAPTER TWO

Fishers, Indiana

Austin Hemple looked at him and asked, "You nervous?"

Brett shrugged, made a face like he didn't have a care in the world, and then shook his head.

"Are you thinking about him?"

Still looking out over the track infield where he and Austin sprawled waiting for the sprint coach to tell the track team to warm up, he answered, "A little."

"Then you're nervous," Austin said.

Brett ignored him. Instead, he leaned down over his legs that were out in front of him, reached with both hands and grabbed his bare feet. His nose touched a spot between his legs, and he held that position for a four count. Then he spread both legs out, stretching them as far to either side as he could, bent at his waist, and stretched out his arms in front of him. His nose nearly touched the grass beneath him.

For a fifth grader, Brett McGovern was put together. A complete package as sports commentators might say about an athlete. He was smart in the classroom when he wanted to be, which was most often. Though Brett was on the short side, he had a six-pack and a broad muscular chest with shoulders to match. He had thick, well-defined thighs, with thin but muscular calves. Sprinter's legs. His skin tone was naturally dark, which in the sun, turned even darker. That was a tribute to his Italian heritage, a gift from his mother and her side of the family.

He took care of his body, which was remarkable for an eleven-year-old, but then again, Brett seemed older and more mature than others of his age. He was cautious in what he ate and drank, because he considered himself an athlete. He knew deep down in every fiber of his being that he was an athlete. He had national times in the 100, the 200, and in the long jump. On top of all that, he was a cute young man.

Everyone told him he and his little brother, Bobby, looked like mini-Tom Brady's, minus the cleft chin. And while most boys his age might have taken that as a compliment, Brett didn't, because his favorite quarterback was and forever would be Payton Manning.

Brett excelled at football, as a running back and safety, and played on an AAU team, out of Indianapolis, called the Bombers. His buddy, Austin, was the quarterback. The two of them also played on an AAU basketball team together, with Brett being the better of the two, but that didn't matter, because Brett and Austin were best friends. In fact, the two were pretty much inseparable.

"Look, there he is."

Brett glanced in the direction Austin was staring.

Da'Shawn Grimes was a seventh grader at a city school in Indy. He was big, muscular, skin the color of dark chocolate, with long dreds that dangled onto his shoulders. He walked in front of a group of his teammates, a girl on his right, a guy on his left. The others laughed at something, but Grimes saw Brett looking at him and stared back. He was so intent on Brett, he didn't respond to whatever was funny, and ignored the shove from the guy on his left.

He stopped, said something to the group, left them, and walked slowly towards Brett.

"Here he comes," Austin whispered.

Grimes stood over Brett, "You McGovern?"

Brett looked up at him, "Yeah. You Grimes?"

He sat down on the grass facing Brett and Austin and began stretching out just as Brett was.

"Austin, I'll catch up with you later, okay?"

Austin stared first at Brett, then at Grimes, and then got up and walked away.

"Dude, what are you racing today?"

"Same as you," Bett said, "The hundred, two hundred, and the four by two."

Da'Shawn nodded. "Dude, I guess we'll be seeing each other a lot today."

"Looks that way."

They stretched in silence for a little while and then Grimes stopped, and leaned back on an elbow. "What's your best sport?"

Truth was, Brett liked everything and didn't really have a favorite. He just liked to compete, liked the challenge, and liked to push himself.

So he said honestly, "I like them all, except baseball. Baseball is a cure insomnia."

Grimes laughed with Brett. "You're pretty smart, aren't you?"

Brett's shrug was his only answer.

Grimes nodded. "I saw you play basketball once or twice. Pretty good. I read about you in football. But track," he stopped, shook his head and smiled, "Dude, you can flat out fly for a white boy."

Brett grinned. "I like them all."

"Except baseball," Grimes said with a laugh.

Brett laughed. "Yeah, except baseball."

"I need to do good, 'cause I gotta get outta here. Dude, I got nothin' here. Nothin'. I gotta do good."

"You have national times, too, Da'Shawn. You're doing really well in track."

"Yeah, but *really well* is only *really well*."

Brett wasn't sure what he meant.

"Dude, look, I gotta get to my team. I'll catch you later, okay?"

Brett knuckle bumped him. "Good luck."

Grimes laughed. "Dude, luck's got nothin' to do with it. But I'll tell you what. When I pass your scrawny white ass, I'll try not to fart in your face."

Brett laughed. "I'd appreciate it, Da'Shawn, but you might not have to worry about that."

CHAPTER THREE

Fishers, Indiana

Tony Dominico, Brett's uncle, stood by the fence and watched his nephew talk to the other kid—the opponent—and he didn't like it at all. Brett should be focusing. He should focus on winning the race and not letting the Grimes kid mess with his mind.

Dominico was an Indianapolis detective in the narcotics squad. Back in the day, like his nephew, he was a star athlete through middle school, high school and in college, at the University of Indiana. At six-two and two hundred and twenty pounds, he still kept himself in shape. Dominico worked out at the gym three or four days a week with free weights. He'd pound a heavy bag every now and then and jump rope for twenty minutes every day. If that wasn't enough, he ran six to ten miles before dawn in any kind of weather. And, it was at his uncle's insistence that Brett begin pumping weights, which is why Brett was as developed as he was.

He knew Brett didn't like pep talks or any rah-rah crap, but Dominico felt he needed to help Brett regain his focus if he was going to beat the Grimes kid. So, he hopped over the fence, crossed the track and walked to the center where Brett sat, stretching with a couple of his teammates.

"Guys, can I talk to my nephew for a minute or two?" he asked, fully expecting the boys to leave, which they did.

When they left, he said, "Brett, what the hell were you thinking talking to that Spade right before you have to race him, huh? What were you thinking?"

Brett glared at him defiantly. "I wasn't thinking anything!"

"Exactly! You weren't thinking at all. You let him get inside your head. What did he do? How awful his life is? Try to get you to feel sorry for him?"

"He didn't do any of that," Brett hissed.

"Don't you understand, Brett? You have a chance to beat this guy. You and he have the best times in the state and two of the best times in the nation. Less than a couple of hundredths of a second separates you two and you can finish him today, right now, if you get your shit together and focus."

Brett fumed. He was so angry, he couldn't respond. He hated anyone talking to him before a race, before a basketball game, before a football game, or before anything. And for his uncle to come onto the track infield, tell his friends to leave, and then start this crap; it was too much.

He grabbed his cleats and stood up. "I'm going to go warm up with my team."

"Brett, listen," Dominico said, reaching out a hand to grab his shoulder.

Brett didn't give him a chance. He turned his back on him. "I have to go."

CHAPTER FOUR

Fishers, Indiana

He watched Brett stretch and warm up. He focused on the beads of sweat on his face, his upper lip and on his neck. He watched the little sweat rivers trail down his arms, from under his arms, and down his legs. When Brett used the front of his shirt to wipe sweat from his face, he was able to see Brett's chest and stomach.

He had been watching Brett grow and had been *interested* in him for a couple of months, perhaps, obsessed with him. He loved Brett's large brown eyes, the way he cut his brown hair, the fullness of his lips. He would focus on the way Brett's muscles would flex when he walked, ran, threw a football or shot a basketball. He seldom missed one of Brett's games, and he was always around, always nearby, watching, hoping, waiting. Best of all, he enjoyed it when he got close to Brett to catch his scent.

Of course, there were other boys, especially in Chicago where he visited as often as he could. He took pleasure in them, with them, but Brett was special. He would watch, and hope, and wait for the right opportunity, the right time.

He knew Brett's little brother, younger by a year and a few months, would grow to be special just like Brett, but Brett was a cut above. Brett was special. He liked Brett's determination, his intensity, even his stubbornness. There was hardness in Brett, whereas, Bobby seemed soft, too soft for his taste, but then again, maybe that would change.

But for now, he would watch, hope, and wait. Brett would be his.

Mostly, he would plan. He was very good at planning.

CHAPTER FIVE

Washington, D.C.

"The boy's name is Richard Clarke, from Flagstaff, Arizona," Summer said tiredly. The group known as Kiddie Corps met in a conference room that wasn't much bigger than a closet. The swivel chairs were padded and comfortable, but they were so jammed up against the long table and walls, they could barely maneuver.

She sat to the right of Logan Musgrave, the section supervisor. Next to her was Douglas Rawson, a tall, thin, elegantly dressed black man who seldom spoke unless he asked a question for clarification. Some in the department suspected he was a beneficiary of affirmative action, but both Pete and Summer liked him and trusted him. He had a good mind. They also knew he was on the ladder climbing to the top, so they didn't know how long they'd actually have him in the unit.

Across from Summer sat the youngest member of the Crimes Against Children Unit, Chet Walker, the computer guy. Some called the red-haired, freckle-faced guy a computer geek, and that wouldn't be far from the truth. Pete liked the kid. He was inquisitive, had a ready sense of humor, filled with sarcasm, worked tirelessly, and in Pete's opinion, was the best computer guy in the FBI. Word had it, Walker could hack into anything or anyone without detection. Rumors also had it that it was because of his hacking ability that he worked for the FBI, so perhaps he wasn't as undetectable as most suspected. Still, he was a good man to have on one's side in any cyber fight.

"How old was he?" Musgrave asked.

"He was eleven-years-old, one month shy of his twelfth birthday when he was taken. He was fourteen when he was found." Storm answered.

"So, he was missing a little over two years." Rawson said.

"This is similar to the other boy... who was that? The kid found in Nevada?" Musgrave asked.

"Brian Mullaney," Pete answered. "Both were shot with a .38 from behind, at close range. Both were found nude with their hands cuffed behind their back.

Both were kneeling at the time they were shot. Both had signs of prolonged sexual abuse." Pete paused, ran his hands over his face and said, "Christ."

"So... we have two boys about the same age, taken from two different states, and murdered at about the same age, but found in two other states from the states they had lived in," Musgrave said reading over his notes.

"Same weapon, same MO," Chet added. "What about the brand?" he asked holding up an eight by ten glossy.

"I ran it by a profiler in Quantico, she said a couple of things," Summer said. "First, the whipping was done with a leather strap. The ME found leather slivers in the wounds. But it wasn't a fresh branding. It was done at some point while the kid was held captive. She felt the whipping could have been some pervert's way of getting off. She also suggested it might be a punishment for something. Second, the brand was likely another punishment, obviously more severe than the whipping. Like an escalation of punishment." Summer shrugged.

"Could this be one perpetrator?" Musgrave asked.

"I doubt it, but possibly, depending on the age, strength, and size of the perpetrator, at least that's what the profiler speculated."

"Was she able to give us a profile of who we're looking for?" Rawson asked.

"Well, we know most pedophiles are white male, twenty to fifty, single, who don't get along well with their own peer group, and who tend to hang around kids of a specific age group and gender, no real friends," Summer answered. "Other than that ..." she trailed off with a shrug.

"Chet, were you able to make any connections between the two boys, any similarities, differences?" Musgrave asked.

Chet shrugged noncommittally. "They weren't related. One kid, Mullaney, had dark hair. Clarke had blond hair. Both were taken at about the same age, and both were murdered at about the same age. Both came from middle class families. Both had at least one sibling. Both boys were athletic, had good grades in school, and were considered by their parents and others as leaders."

"So, we don't really have much," Rawson said.

"We have squat," Pete said.

"Technically, we can't call this a serial yet, because we need three victims, points of reference," Summer said. "But if you look at the death scenes, the MO, the ME reports, the position of the bodies, the weapon, and the handcuffs...

taking all that together, I think it's just a matter of time before we find another body, and it will be just like the other two."

"Shit!" Chet said, just loud enough for everyone to hear, but not realizing he said it out loud.

That, however, summed up the feeling from everyone sitting around the table.

CHAPTER SIX

Reston, Virginia

The man looked over his shoulder, then across the street in both directions, and then as nonchalantly as he could, punched in the numbers using a disposable, untraceable phone, in order to make the call.

"They found two bodies so far," he stepped on a bug, a beetle of some sort, grinding it into the sidewalk using the toe of his expensive shoe.

"What do they know?"

"Not much… yet, but it's just a matter of time before they begin putting things together," he answered glancing left and right as if he were bored with the conversation, but taking in any passersby, anyone who might be watching him.

"Can you steer them away from us?"

"I don't think so, especially not if they find another body."

"Who's working the case?"

"Kelliher and Storm, and they're good."

"How good?"

"Very. Kelliher is a cop. Thorough, precise. Storm is sharp, and scary smart, almost as good a cop as Kelliher."

"What do you suggest?"

"Tell them to find a better location for disposal. One that's not in the open, one that will be more… discreet, hidden. A site where the elements and critters can help with the disposal. I'll monitor the investigation as best I can, but I have to be careful."

"I pay you to be careful."

"Yeah, well," he answered, wanting the phone call to end.

"I'll pass it on. Keep in touch."

"Will do."

The man ended the call, slipped the phone into his pocket, and pretended to window shop, but used the reflection in the glass to see behind him. No one sat in cars. No one paid any attention to him. Whatever foot traffic was on the street, kept moving this way and that, same with the passing cars.

Safe and unsuspected, for now, but he'd have to keep it that way.

CHAPTER SEVEN

Fishers, Indiana

Fortunately for Brett, his team drew the even lanes, so Cosby Middle School from the city would have to run in the odd lanes. Brett didn't like lane one, not that he had ever had to run in it. He didn't like to be on the outside edge, but instead, he liked the middle, because he could see who was where. Not overly superstitious, Brett liked even numbered lanes and preferred to run from lane four, which was where he set up his starting block.

He hadn't spoken much to anyone since his uncle climbed up his ass. He was still pissed off about that, but he had regained his focus. As he got ready for the sprint, he slowed his breathing and cleared his mind. From his vantage point, the track, one hundred meters of it anyway, was nothing but a straightaway, like an airport runway, waiting for him to begin his approach and take off. Except, airport runways weren't made of rubberized turf.

Grimes lined up in lane three, just to Brett's left. They hadn't spoken and Brett preferred it that way. He could see the tenseness in Grimes' face, the tautness of the thick muscle in his legs and arms. Brett dismissed it, all of it. He had one goal, one. That's all he thought about. That was the only thing on his mind.

Brett studied the Starter trying to learn his rhythm. He thought he had it down, especially, between the "get set" and the Starter's gun. He wondered if Grimes had done the same, because the finish could actually come down to who started the fastest, since they were only three hundredths of a second separating the two of them.

He climbed into his block, stretched, shook out his right leg, and then did the same to his left, and then relaxed into a semi-crouch. He was ready for the starter's instructions and the gun. Like most sprinters, Brett used his fingertips for balance. His coach and his uncle had differed in how much pressure to place on them, with his uncle wanting more pressure, while his coach wanted less. Brett resisted the coaching from his uncle, because he was comfortable with less pressure. He also didn't like being told what to do. Besides, it had worked for him so far, so he didn't see the need for changing the way he positioned himself in the block.

"Runners to your marks!"

Brett and Grimes were ready, while the other sprinters fidgeted.

"Set!"

The runners balanced on legs and fingers, and most but not all, looked down. Both Grimes and Brett looked down. Both boys knew that the winner would be the one who could get to their top speed the quickest and hold it the longest. Brett intended to be that sprinter. He had no doubt Da'Shawn Grimes had the same intention.

The gun went off and both Brett and Grimes blasted out of their blocks while the other runners were still set. By the ten yard mark, Brett and Grimes were even and well ahead of the pack. They knew it was a two-man race. So, did everyone in the stands.

At the fifty- and seventy-five-meter marks, they were still even, and neither were straining. Feet flew. Arms and legs pumped in precise motion. Brett had more lean, while Grimes was more up and down.

At the finish, it looked to everyone like a tie. Looked like a tie. The clock told a different story.

CHAPTER EIGHT

Washington, D.C.

"Pete, we just got word that another body was found." Summer said, "This time, in Michigan." She hadn't realized just how hard she clutched her phone.

Pete sighed, a hand running over his face that ended up on his flattop. He didn't have to ask who. He didn't have to ask if it was their case. Like Summer, he just knew. But then the significance of what she said kicked in.

"Wait! What? Michigan?"

"A remote area near a small town called White Cloud. A fourteen-year-old boy was found. Same MO. Handcuffs, nude, two gunshots to the back of the head. Looks to be from a .38."

"Jesus! Michigan, what the hell! Nevada, California, now *Michigan?*"

"Wheels up in thirty minutes."

"Is the scene secure?"

"State Police and the Detroit FBI office are on it.

Pete paced in his office with one hand securely holding his phone, the other on top of his head.

"Summer, if this is the same circumstance and situation as the other two sites..."

"Then we have a serial."

"But in two different parts of the country? Happening at the same time? This might mean . . ."

"More than one perp, maybe, but we don't know the timing on this one, compared to the other two boys who were found. It could be that the perp started in one area and is moving to another area."

"Yeah, maybe, but you don't believe that, like I don't believe that. We have more than one perp."

"Pete, we have to get out in front of this thing and we have to do it in a hurry. I hate that we're behind."

"See you in thirty."

CHAPTER NINE

Fishers, Indiana

Brett crossed the finish line and ran another thirty yards, jogged another fifteen, then walked back still in his lane. Grimes was at the finish line, bent over at the waist, a grimace on his face, breathing hard and deep.

Brett's sprint coach, Robbie Coleman, met him at the line, but away from Grimes and the others.

"Well, I have good news and bad news."

"I lost, didn't I?"

Coleman smiled sadly, "Bottom line? Yes, you lost, but only by five thousandths of a second. You also had a PR, and as fast as you are, a personal record at the end of April is hard to get."

Brett frowned. "What was my time?"

"You hit eleven point five one. That's point fourteen seconds faster than last week, Brett, and like I said, it's only the end of April. You keep improving this quickly, and you could be hitting the high tens at the end of May."

Brett nodded and shrugged dismissively.

Coleman put a hand on Brett's shoulder. "Brett, listen to me, okay? You're the fastest kid I've ever coached. I doubt I'll ever coach anyone as fast as you ever again. You went up against a kid who is just as fast as you."

"He's faster."

Coleman nodded. "Yes, by five thousandths of a second. Do you realize how small a margin that is? And think of this. He's in seventh grade. You're in fifth. He's well into his growth spurt, and you've barely begun. He is going to plateau out, probably in high school, before you ever hit your peak. That's a big deal. That's something to remember, because you still have to race him in the four by two and in the two hundred meters," he paused. "As hard as it might be, you need to put this behind you pretty quickly, because you and your three team members are about to race."

Brett wiped his face off with the front of his shirt, nodded, walked away and found Grimes standing, watching him with both of his hands resting on top of his head.

"Nice race, Da'Shawn."

JOSEPH LEWIS 19

"For a white boy, you can really fly," he repeated, shaking his head.

Brett smiled and said, "Well, wait until you see me in the two hundred," and he walked away to join his teammates at the start of the relay.

Grimes watched him walk away and then muttered, "Shit!"

CHAPTER TEN

East of Round Rock, Navajo Indian Reservation, Arizona

Tending sheep was boring. There were long stretches of nothing but watching jackrabbits, dust devils, and the sun advancing from one horizon to the other, while protecting his family's herd from coyotes or from rustlers. Rustlers were actually more common than coyotes.

Like his grandfather had taught him, George Tokay sat among the pinion pine and Joshua trees on the side of the mountain. His horse was tied behind the ridge on the other side of the stand of pines. Across his lap were a loaded Winchester .22, a canteen, and binoculars. In his saddlebag was some jerky that would tie him over until supper. His saddlebag also contained an apple, and a carrot for the big, black wild stallion he was trying to befriend.

His day began before dawn, up on a mesa, overlooking his family's humble, if not poor, little ranch, with his grandfather, who taught him the Navajo language, along with the traditional prayers and songs of the Navajo people. In less than one month, George would turn twelve in a coming of age ceremony on that same mesa. In the Navajo culture, the day one comes of age is an important day, at least to the traditional Navajo, like George and his family. He would receive his Navajo *name* that would only be known to him and his grandfather, unless George chose to share it with others. It was up to him, but frowned upon if not discouraged.

After greeting Father Sun, George and his grandfather headed back to the ranch, where he cleaned up, ate a simple breakfast, and along with his brother, William, younger by eighteen months, caught the bus for school.

Their ranch consisted of a three-bedroom hogan. One bedroom was for his grandparents, one was for his mother and sister, who shared the bed, and one for George and his two brothers, the three of them crowded into the same bed. The only other rooms were a kitchen and a family room. The house was made of wood and heated by a fireplace. His mother and grandmother would cook over a wood stove inside, or if the weather was good, outside, and the weather was mostly good. The only other buildings were an outhouse, set back from the house, and a barn that had gaps where wood either rotted or fallen away. There wasn't running water, electricity, or a phone. But the extended family who lived there was happy and healthy.

George wore his black hair long, well past his shoulders. As often as he could, he spoke the Navajo language, mostly with his grandparents and his mother, and with an older science teacher at the school. George was also fluent in both Spanish and English.

After school and after grabbing a quick snack- if there was one- he would saddle up one of two horses, fill his canteen from the well, check his rifle to make sure it was loaded, and grab some rope for a wandering lamb or sheep, though they pretty much stayed together as they grazed on the side of the hill.

When the wild stallion came over the top of the rise to graze along with the sheep, George would take the apple and the carrot and approach the big black horse, slowly, cautiously, and talking to it gently and softly. The closest the horse would allow him to approach so far, was about ten yards, before it would whinny and back off. When the horse did that, George would place the apple and carrot on the ground and back slowly away, still talking quietly and softly, anything to get the horse used to him. It seemed to be working. At least, that was what George thought.

While he watched the sheep, he would usually read books. Any mystery by *Tony Hillerman* was his usual fare, but lately he practiced the songs and prayers his grandfather had taught him, because he wanted the coming of age ceremony to be perfect. He didn't want to disappoint his grandfather.

Secretly, he wanted to be like his grandfather, who was a holy man, a *singer*, among the Navajo people, the *Dine'*, and who had the reputation of being similar to an archbishop or cardinal in the Roman Catholic religion. He knew this because many of his people converted to this faith, something neither he nor his family had done or would do. But his grandfather was that important. The *biligaana*, or white man, might refer to him as a Medicine Man, or in Navajo, a *Haatalii*, and they would not be wrong. The Navajo elders referred to him as *Hosteen* Tokay, a term of respect. But his grandfather was that important. George wanted to learn the songs and had hoped to one day become a *singer*, like his grandfather.

Spring in the desert was not nearly as hot or dry as the desert was in summer, but it was still hot and fairly dry just the same. Growing up in the desert and having never left the reservation, George knew how to take care of himself. Plenty of shade, plenty of water, and a beat up straw cowboy hat that was a gift from his mother to shield his face. He seldom wore a shirt, but instead wore a leather vest, a pair of jeans, and his cowboy boots, though he always brought his moccasins with him. And when all of that failed, there was a stream over the rise and down in the valley that cooled him off if it had recently rained, or if there had been snow up in the mountains and on the mesas and if the runoff had made it down that far.

George liked his life, though he knew no other way of living. And he loved his family, especially his grandfather. He had never really known his father who used to come around every so often, and then leave for great stretches of time. But ever since the birth of his sister, the youngest member of his family, he had left and hadn't returned, and no one seemed to think he would. George didn't mind or care about his father, but he did worry if his mother was happy. To him, she seemed to be, though she would never complain if she wasn't happy.

At school, George excelled in and loved history and science, and was only fair in math and English grammar. He loved the reading, just didn't do well with the grammar. By nature, he was quiet and would rather observe, so he typically listened to his classmates and the teacher, though he would ask questions if he didn't understand something and would answer questions if called upon. But generally, he preferred to listen and watch, and he was very good at listening and watching.

His dream, not that he had ever shared it with anyone—not even his grandfather—was to become a crime scene investigator, and work for the Navajo Tribal Police, just like his cousin, Leonard. Perhaps in time, he would be able to join the FBI, even though they didn't have a great reputation among the Navajo people, especially among the Navajo police, with whom there seemed to be jurisdictional issues and conflicts. At least that was what his cousin said when he came to visit.

According to his cousin, crimes on the reservation consisted of drugs and alcohol related offenses. Domestic conflicts, car theft, cattle rustling, and an occasional fight or two, usually after someone drank too much. Sometimes, there was a murder and his cousin said it was usually over drugs. Oxycontin, cocaine, and heroin were the drugs of choice on the rez, along with marijuana. Most everyone on the rez was poor. Money seemed to land in very few pockets, other than into a big rancher's pocket who had a lot of land for cattle or sheep. Sometimes big money was made illegally by selling prescription narcotics, especially since legitimate jobs were scarce.

George's grandfather blamed the *biligaana*, white people, for that. But his grandfather told George and his brother that even though the *biligaana* were to blame, the *Dine'* still had a choice whether or not to take part in that. His grandfather would often say that there were two coyotes living in each of us. One is good and the other is bad. Whichever one we feed is the one who lives. He would then turn to George and ask, '*Which coyote will you feed today?*' And George would always answer the good coyote. His grandfather, still expressionless, would nod, and that would be the end of the conversation.

George smiled as he pictured his grandfather looking off in the distance, no expression on his face. His grandfather would often tell him that a true Navajo would never betray one's feelings by showing emotion.

Quietly, moving subtly and slowly, George checked his rifle, moving his finger onto the trigger lightly, though he was pretty certain he knew who it was.

"It took you long enough."

"I knew you were there," George said. "I could smell your hair."

Rebecca Morning Star stepped out from among the pines and faced him, then looked out over the sheep.

George stood up next to her, waiting for her to say something. He had known Rebecca and her brother, Charles, since early elementary school. Their families were from different clans. Rebecca's family was from the *To'ahani* or the Near The Water Clan, while George's family was from the *'Azee'tsoh dine'e* which translated to The Big Medicine People Clan. But their ranches were within three miles of each other and they went to the same school. Rebecca and George were both in fifth grade, while Charles was in sixth, and the three of them, along with George's younger brother, William, hunted together, rode together, camped together, and when possible, and if there was a need, helped each other with their chores.

Rebecca was a female mirror image of George, bronze skin that turned dark brown in the desert summer sun. Both had a near noble look, he was handsome, she was pretty. Both were the same height and on the skinny side. They were athletic. Although neither played on nor had time for organized sports. They were best friends and George had only recently begun wondering if Rebecca liked him as more than just a friend.

"Do you ever get tired watching sheep?"

"No, not really," George said, pushing his cowboy hat up off his brow.

She was silent for a bit, and then folded her arms across her chest and asked, "Do you think we'll ever get off the rez?"

The first answer that came to George was that he doubted it, but he was also pretty sure that he didn't really want to leave the rez. *Where would he... they... go?*

So, he safely said, "I don't know."

Rebecca sat down on some rocks that had a shape of a chair, exactly where George sat earlier.

"Do you have any jerky?"

"In the saddlebag. There's water in the canteen if you're thirsty."

Rebecca dug around in the bag, took out a small piece, and nibbled on it.

George sat down on the desert sand next to her and offered her the canteen, but she shook her head.

From the corner of his eyes, he studied her. Her full lips, narrow nose, large dark eyes with long lashes, shiny long black hair. He knew she was smart. She could also ride a horse as well or better than most boys, and was an excellent shot. Like George, she was quiet and watched, observed, and listened.

Her breasts, which for a fifth grader and compared to the other girls in his class, were large.

Even though she was in fifth grade, she looked and acted more mature than any of the other fifth grade girls. But as his mother would often say, things seemed to happen faster on the rez than they do elsewhere. From what he could tell as he dressed out in the locker room for physical education, even George had begun developing faster than many boys his age.

Rebecca stood up, so George did too. She dusted sand off of her legs, placed her hands on her hips and said, "Can I ask you a question?"

George nodded.

"We will officially be sixth graders in four weeks. Two days after that, you turn twelve."

George said nothing, not knowing where this was headed.

"You're so smart in school, but you're so dumb in life."

George's mouth opened and he wanted to protest, but remained silent instead.

"Why is it you can't figure out that I want you to kiss me? Is it just you who is that slow or are all boys from the Big Medicine Clan that slow?"

"I... I..." George stuttered, not knowing what he should say.

Instead, Rebecca stepped over to him, pushed his hat off his head and onto the ground. She placed both arms around his neck and kissed him, long and deeply, and passionately, her mouth open, her tongue gentle on his. She held the kiss a long time, pulled back, and then did it again, this time, softer and longer; her body pressing into his.

It took George by complete surprise, but he did manage to hold her gently around her waist. He had no choice but to kiss her back, cursing himself, because he didn't know if he was doing it correctly, having never kissed a girl before. He did feel a stirring that he had never felt before, and he liked that feeling.

She pulled back, stared at him, allowing George to see her—perhaps for the first time—and then started to walk away. George stared at her, not moving.

"When you figure it out, let me know," Rebecca said with her back to him as she walked through the pines to her horse.

CHAPTER ELEVEN

Fishers, Indiana

Brett had already won the long jump on only his second attempt with an 18' 11", bettering his jump from the previous week of 17' 6", and he still had one attempt to go.

However, he wasn't even thinking about it. Instead, he was concentrating on the two-hundred-meter race. He and his three teammates got killed in the four by two hundred. While Brett, Austin Hemple and Brian Green were fast, their second leg runner, Mike Lowry, was the weakest of the four runners. Brett at least managed to keep pace with his anchor split from the previous week, but by the time Green handed off to him, he was already ten yards behind Grimes.

Brett went in search of Lowry, who had walked off by himself. He found him stretching in the infield away from everyone.

"Mike, you okay?"

Lowry shrugged and kept his head down. "I suck!"

"Yeah, you suck, but you're still pretty fast," Brett teased.

Lowry looked up at him. "I'm the slowest one in the four by two."

"But you're still faster than anyone else who could fill that spot," he paused to let that sink in and then added, "Coach was pretty happy. You had a PR , so you should be too."

"But we still lost."

"But as a team, we improved and got faster."

Lowry shrugged.

"So, shake it off, okay? I need you at the one hundred meter mark to tell me how far Grimes is behind me."

Lowry got up and walked across the infield with Brett.

"Who says Grimes will be behind you?" Lowry asked.

Brett smiled. "You really do suck, Mike!" and gave him a shove for emphasis and both boys ended up laughing.

The lane assignments were the same as the one hundred meter, with Grimes in lane three and Brett in lane four, but because a turn was involved, Grimes was in his starting block behind Brett.

Before getting into his block, Brett bent over at the waist, and, keeping his legs straight, touched his toes. Then he spread his legs and touched his nose to his right leg, then to his left. He mounted himself into his block, shook out first his right leg, set it, and then shook out his left, and then settled in to wait for the starter's instructions.

"Runners to your marks!"

Brett was certain Grimes was already set, just as he was.

"Set!"

And Brett timed the starter just right once again and shot out of his block, low, hard and fast. As they took the curve, Brett was ahead of everyone in lanes five through eight. He had a suspicion that Grimes was about even with him, and that proved to be correct.

At the fifty yard mark, Brett was ahead by at least four steps. He saw Lowry at the one hundred yard mark and heard him yell.

"Three yards!"

At the one-fifty yard mark, he and Grimes were almost side by side, though Brett still kept a one or two step lead. But Grimes was big, strong and fast.

At the one hundred seventy-five yard mark, Brett had visions of a repeat of the one hundred meter race, because Grimes had pulled even.

Both boys were determined to win. Neither boy wanted to come in second, regardless of a PR time. Brett leaned into the finish and to any spectator, it looked as though it was a tie.

But once again, the clock told a different story.

CHAPTER TWELVE

White Cloud, Michigan

Both Pete and Summer were road weary. Three days, two different states, and dead bodies in each, and now a total of three dead bodies in three states. Three bodies of children, all boys.

Pete stood up from examining the brown-haired boy, looked into the trees, and then at the sky, hoping one scene or the other would erase the vision of the boy that lay on the ground, dead, before him. Summer had already turned her back and was on the phone to the National Center for Missing Children, following up on the picture she sent of the boy earlier. As she talked, she paced with one hand holding the cell and the other on her hip.

"Let me know when you have an ID, okay?" And then a second or so later, Summer said, "And any other information you can provide such as the day, month and year of the boy's abduction, his age at the time of abduction, and the city and state of residence." And still a beat or two later, Summer added, "You have my number. I'll wait for your call. Thanks."

She slipped the phone into the pocket of her black slacks and walked a short distance away, knowing Pete would follow.

"The ME said the time of death was within twenty-four hours."

"I heard him," Summer said wearily.

"I think we need to reevaluate what we have and perhaps come up with a different theory."

Summer didn't even want to consider any other theory, but she knew Pete was correct.

Pete didn't do laptops or iPads or any other electronics, except for his smart phone, so he pulled out the little notebook that seemed to live in his sport coat pocket. Chet and the other members of Kiddie Corps teased him, by calling it *"The Pete Kelliher 2014."* Pete opened it up and pushed the pages back to the first boy found in Nevada.

"Just to recap what we already know... Brian Mullaney from California, had dark hair and no brand on his ankle. Richard Clarke from Flagstaff, Arizona had blond hair and a brand on his left ankle. An upside-down cross. He was also whipped with a leather strap."

He paused, looked at Summer. She was visibly pale, her hair was mussed up, and she had dark half-circles under both eyes.

"This kid is about the same age as the other two boys. This kid has brown hair. There are no whip marks and there is no brand. All three boys were found with their hands cuffed behind their backs. All three were found with two shots to the back of the head. We know in the case of the first two boys, Mullaney and Clarke, a .38 was used and I'm willing to bet that a .38 was used on this boy. I'm also willing to bet that the bullets found in this boy will match the bullets taken from Mullaney and Clarke. And, I'm also willing to bet that just as in the case of both Mullaney and Clarke, this boy was sexually abused over a long period of time."

"Looks like we have a serial, a pedophile."

Pete bit the inside of this mouth before speaking.

"What?" Summer asked.

"Given the time frame of the other two boys, and then adding this boy, and factoring in the locations of all three boys, we've got to consider that there is something bigger going on, something that might involve more than one pedophile. This isn't random. It doesn't feel random. It feels planned. It feels thought out. It feels organized. It feels deliberate."

"So, what are you suggesting?" Summer said.

Pete shook his head and sighed.

"I'm not sure yet, so I don't want to hazard a guess. I certainly don't want to put any theories out there yet. I want to find out more about this boy, and I want to factor in everything we know about Mullaney and Clarke. Then, I want to get Chet and his computer revved up. Before we say or do anything... before we bring this to the whole group, we have to think this through, you and me first."

And then, as he turned his back on her and looked once more at the ME, kneeling over the dead boy, he ran a hand over his mostly gray flattop and muttered, "Fuck me!"

30 TAKING LIVES

CHAPTER THIRTEEN

Fishers, Indiana

Just like he did after each race, Brett ran some extra yards, jogged even more, then turned and walked back to the finish line. Once again, Grimes was already there, but was down on one knee, his face contorted into a grimace. Brett's sprint coach, Robbie Coleman, stood talking to the race official and scribbled something on his finals tally sheet, on the clipboard.

Brett stood next to him and peered at the sheet.

"Another PR, Brett, you ran a twenty- one- point fifty- four. You took two- point twenty- nine seconds off your time. Dang, Brett, you were flying!"

"Did I win or lose?"

"You won by two thousandths of a second."

Brett beamed, pumped a fist in the air, and shouted, "Yes!"

Grimes had gotten to his feet, but was bent over at the waist, with his hands on his hips. He straightened up with his hands on the top of his head, gulping in air.

"Nice race, Da'Shawn," Brett said patting him on the back.

Grimes, being a head taller, slung an arm across Brett's shoulders. "Shit, McGovern. I never had to run as hard as I did today. Damn, dude!"

Brett smiled, gave him a shove, and they both laughed.

CHAPTER FOURTEEN

Fishers, Indiana

He stood for the entire track meet and perhaps more than anyone else. He was relieved that Brett had won the two-hundred meter. Still, it was too close.

However, he didn't like the fact that Brett was so friendly with the other boy, his opponent. He didn't like it all.

He enjoyed it when Brett used the front of his jersey to wipe off his face. He could see Brett's stomach, his muscles. He liked looking at Brett's face, his smile, and his chestnut-colored eyes. He liked watching Brett flex his arm muscles and his leg muscles when he ran.

He must have taken thirty or forty pictures of Brett. He'd have to cull and pick the ones that were truly worthy of showing who Brett was, because only those that were truly worthy would make it into his gallery. He might even share one or two with Brett and his parents. It was unfortunate Brett's parents were such simpletons, such nobodies who didn't truly appreciate Brett, who could never truly appreciate Brett. Certainly not like he could.

Now, what to do with the boy that beat Brett? What should he do about Grimes?

CHAPTER FIFTEEN

Indianapolis, Indiana
It wasn't hard for him to follow Grimes home.

All he had to do was follow a big yellow school bus to Crosby Middle School, and then wait until Grimes came out of the school, near the gym and locker room area, near the parking lot. Then, he followed a block or so behind him and three other track athletes. The lone girl among them hung closely at Grimes' side, touching his arm, his shoulder, and his hand as the group talked and laughed.

There was nothing quiet about them. Everything was at the top of their lungs, mouths open in a half-yell, acting like clowns.

He didn't have any respect for them, none.

First, one boy would peel off and head down a different street, then another. Finally, the girl left, clearly wanting Grimes to display some affection—a kiss, a hug, hold her hand—but he didn't. Grimes was either not interested in her or didn't catch on to what the girl wanted.

It confirmed to him that Grimes was as stupid as he suspected him to be.

As she finally headed down a different street, Grimes was walking alone, ear buds in his ears, listening to some hip- hop crap, he was sure.

He drove ahead, turned right, then left and then left again, so Grimes would be walking right towards him. He parked and waited until the boy was twenty yards away, and then got out of the car.

As Grimes approached, he said, "Da'Shawn? Da'Shawn Grimes?"

Wary, not sure what a white man was doing in that part of the neighborhood, Grimes slowed his walking, hesitated, and looked for an escape route.

"I was just at the track meet and saw you run. You are an incredible runner."

Grimes smiled, blushed. "Thank you!" as he continued walking towards him.

As Grimes was within two feet of him, he said, "Just one thing, Da'Shawn. You should never have beaten Brett McGovern, and I'm going to make sure you never beat him again."

Grimes stopped. His arms hung at his sides. On his back was his backpack. In his right hand was his athletic bag. Da'Shawn saw the gun appear out of the man's pocket. He recognized a silencer.

The gun spit once, twice, and then a third time. All shots hit him in the chest, centered over his heart. He was dead before he dropped on his back, almost in front of his house.

The man walked over to the boy lying on the sidewalk and put one last shot into the boy's forehead, and then he calmly got into his car and drove away.

Brett would never lose a race to Da'Shawn Grimes again.

CHAPTER SIXTEEN

Washington, D.C.
Pete, Summer and Chet sat in the Kiddie Corps conference room, on a conference call, with Jack Monahan of the Center For Missing and Sexually Exploited Children. Chet pecked away on his computer, while Pete and Summer jotted down notes on yellow pads.

"The biggest study we have, occurred in nineteen ninety-nine, and here's what we found," Monahan said, sounding as if he was reading from notes. "Approximately eight-hundred-thousand children younger than age eighteen were reported missing. Of those, more than two-hundred-thousand children were abducted by family members. More than fifty-eight-thousand children were abducted by nonfamily members. An estimated one-hundred and fifteen children were the victims of stereotypical kidnapping."

"What are stereotypical kidnappings?" Chet asked.

"Stereotypical kidnappings involved someone the child did not know, or was an acquaintance. The child was held overnight, transported fifty miles or more, killed, ransomed or held with the intent to keep the child permanently."

"Jesus!" Chet said. "I had no idea."

"As you know, the first three hours are the most critical when trying to locate a missing child."

"I thought it was twenty-four to forty-eight hours," Summer said.

"Used to be. Statistics show we needed to narrow the critical time period. An older study told us girls were more than likely found dead in two weeks after their abduction by a stranger, boys generally six months or more."

"Jack, we have three dead boys, all with the same MO," Pete said.

"Well, based upon recent studies, I can tell you that the murder of an abducted child is actually pretty rare. The same study estimated that there are one hundred cases in which an abducted child is murdered in the U.S. each year."

"One hundred kids abducted and murdered, doesn't sound very rare to me," Summer said with disgust. "It sounds like a hell of a lot of kids."

Monahan didn't argue with her, in fact, he agreed with her. His own opinion was that one murdered kid who was abducted was one too many.

"I can tell you that a two-thousand and six study indicated that seventy-six point-two percent of abducted children, who are killed, are dead within three hours of the abduction, and that the National Center has assisted law enforcement in the recovery of more than one-hundred ninety-three thousand, seven-hundred and six missing children since it was founded in nineteen-eighty-four. Our recovery rate for missing children has actually grown from sixty-two percent in nineteen-ninety to ninety-seven percent today."

Pete and Summer sat at the table, digesting the information Monahan had given them. They wrote on their pads of paper, fidgeted in their seats, or drummed their pens as they thought. Chet stared blankly at his computer and shook his head in disbelief.

"Hello? Are you still there?" Monahan asked as the silence grew.

"Yes, we're here," Summer answered sadly. "It's just so much to comprehend. We're talking about kids here, kids who should be playing basketball, or going to school, or having a crush on a boy or girl, and having sleepovers and going to movies. What kind of animal..." she let the question drift, knowing there wasn't an adequate answer for it.

"Jack, the three boys we've found... there was evidence of prolonged sexual abuse," Pete said. "Do you have any information on that?"

"Here is what I can share with you," Monahan said. "The ICAC—"

"What's the ICAC?" Chet asked.

"The Internet Crimes Against Children Task Force," Monahan answered. "The ICAC found more than a one-thousand percent increase in complaints of child sex trafficking from two-thousand-four to two-thousand-eight."

"Jesus Christ!" Chet said, "My God!"

"I know. It's pretty scary," Monahan said.

"I'm going to ask you to go out on a limb, Jack. I know it may not be your area of expertise, but I'm going to give you the information we have on the three boys that were found, and I'd like your opinion."

"I can try," Monahan answered tentatively.

Pete took out his little notebook and gave him the information he and Summer talked about earlier, and had shared with Chet. Summer helped Pete fill in the blanks.

"Hmmm... I don't know. Really, if someone had a gun to my head and asked me what I thought, well, and I have to say that this is only an uneducated guess... I'd say you're dealing with human trafficking. In this case, prepubescent and pubescent boys."

"But given the ages of the boys we've found," Chet said, "they're roughly the same age."

"That isn't atypical," Monahan said. "Pedophiles are age and sex specific. They only stray away from their preferred... choice... if that particular child isn't available. It sounds like, in this case, whoever is taking these kids, wants boys who are prepubescent and then when they reach puberty, they aren't as attractive... for the lack of a better word, so they dispose of them."

Chet rocked back in his chair with his hands on his head.

Summer and Pete stared at one another, trying to read each other's thoughts or perhaps more likely, *reading* each other's thoughts. It was Summer who nodded at Pete.

Pete said, "Jack, I'm going to share with you some information that I ask you not share."

"Okay," Monahan answered cautiously.

"We have two kids found in the Western United States, one in Nevada, the other in Southern California, but in the High Desert area. And then, most recently, a boy was found in Michigan."

"I think I know what you're going to ask me, and the scary answer?" he paused and then said, "I think you're probably dealing with a human trafficking ring that abducts and uses boys."

"I'm going to be sick..." Chet muttered.

CHAPTER SEVENTEEN

Washington, D.C.
"The boy in White Cloud, Michigan is Robert Monroe, from Terre Haute, Indiana. There were no signs of being whipped and there was no brand," Summer had been reading from her notes. She looked up, drank from a bottle of water, and then continued without making eye contact with anyone. "He was one month past his twelfth birthday, and he was fourteen and three months at his death. Two shots to the back of his head with a thirty-eight. Ballistics matched the bullets from the other two boys. Same gun, so, we think it was the same shooter."

"I'm assuming all other characteristics between the three boys were the same?" Logan asked.

"Exactly the same," Chet said. "The boys were nude, kneeling down, hands cuffed, and shot from behind. The three kids were on the honor roll at school and were considered leaders. They were athletes, and had at least one sibling of intact families. You know, their parents are or were together."

Summer and Pete tag-teamed the group with the information they received from the conference call with Monahan of the National Center.

When they were finished, the group was silent. Musgrave folded his hands under his chin as he glanced from Pete to Summer, much like he was watching a tennis match. Rawson sat rigidly upright in his chair, every so often leaning forward to jot down a note or two, but that was seldom. Mostly he listened with his eyes on his note pad, while jiggling his pen between his thumb and forefinger. Chet never took his eyes off his computer screen. He wasn't typing. He didn't look up any internet sites. He just sat still, and stared at it.

"So, what's your theory?" Musgrave finally asked.

Pete and Summer exchanged a look. They decided ahead of this meeting that Pete would do the talking, but both had agreed on what he was going to put forth. They hadn't briefed Chet, and Pete knew he or Summer would have to talk with him after the meeting.

"Like Monahan suspects, I believe we're looking at human trafficking. He suggested, and I agree with him that in this case, someone, a pedophile, or a group of pedophiles, are trafficking prepubescent and pubescent boys. We don't know who. We don't know how. We don't know where. We don't have the answers to any of those questions; yet. But that's what I believe."

Rawson set his pen down on the pad of paper. "But, until you have those answers, or at least one or two of the answers to those questions, you can't be certain."

Pete nodded. "You're correct."

"So, what good will that theory do us in the long run, Pete?" Musgrave asked.

"Not much, I'm afraid."

Musgrave shook his head, pushed back his chair, and stood up.

"So, what you're telling me… us… is that what we actually know for sure is that we have three dead boys who all died the same. We have someone disposing them and killing them with a thirty- eight, in remote areas of the country."

Pete nodded.

"It could be one or two pedophiles who snatch kids off the street, use them for a time, and then dispose of them," Musgrave continued.

"You asked me what my theory was and I gave it to you, based upon the information we do have."

Musgrave shook his head. "I thought you'd have a theory that was somewhat reasonable. Something we can verify one way or the other. I don't believe we have a human trafficking ring. I believe we have one or two pedophiles, snatching and using boys."

"How would that be possible?" Chet said. "You have three kids who were found days apart from one another, in three different states, all dead within an impossible time frame that precludes anything but a human trafficking ring."

"How is that impossible?" Rawson asked.

Chet shook his head in exasperation. "How is that *impossible; seriously*?"

"Chet, settle down," Summer said quietly.

"It's impossible because if it is just one or two guys snatching kids off the street… to use your words, Logan," Pete said, "That would mean these one or two guys are holding three boys together, and who take the time to travel to three different states and dispose of these kids before they decide to go and snatch more kids off the street, again, to use your words. And when they're done with these new kids, these one or two pedophiles will travel the country to, oh, I don't know, three or four other states and dispose of them too. How does that make any more sense than what I'm suggesting?"

"You're bordering on insolence, Pete."

"Yeah, well, I just examined three dead boys in three states, who had signs of prolonged sexual abuse and who were disposed of like someone would dispose of a banana peel or an aluminum can. Sorry if I sound insolent, Logan."

"That's enough!" Logan barked. He stacked his file on his notepad, and started for the door, but stopped and turned around. "One way or the other, Summer, get some better information and try solving this thing before you tell anyone else Pete's theory." With that, he stormed out of the conference room.

Rawson glanced at Pete, then at Summer, and then gathered his things and left the conference room without a word, leaving Summer, Pete and Chet sitting in the conference room.

"That went well, don't you think?" Pete asked.

CHAPTER EIGHTEEN

Arlington, Virginia
The man walked down the street as if he didn't have a care in the world. Stopped at a corner newsstand, bought a paper, then stopped at a street vending cart and bought a Coke, all while watching for any signs that he had been tailed.

Once he was satisfied that he wasn't being watched by anyone, he stood with his back to the street and pretended to window shop, while using the window as a mirror. He kept watch on passerby's cars on the street that had one or more individuals in them. He didn't see any nor did he notice any passersby who paid any particular attention to him.

He tucked the folded newspaper under his arm and held the phone in one hand, while he held the can of Coke in the other.

"Kelliher and Storm have begun putting it together, but they are missing certain key elements and parts to the puzzle."

"How close are they?" came the voice on the other end of the line.

"Hmmm... not very."

"So, we don't have much to worry about yet."

"No, not yet."

"Can you slow them down, maybe, discredit them?"

The man using the window as a mirror to see behind him chuckled, and then said, "I think they're doing a fine job themselves. I don't have to do anything, yet."

"You'll keep monitoring the situation, though, closely?"

"Yes, I will, closely."

"Please, stay in touch, especially if something new comes up."

"I will. Just tell those two to do a better job of disposal."

"I have done that already, and I'll pass it on once again."

"Do that. And, I'll be in touch."

He ended the call, slipped the phone in his pocket, and continued his stroll down the street. He also decided that after the next call, he was going to ask for more money. For the protection and information he was supplying.

CHAPTER NINETEEN

Washington, D.C.

Summer found Chet in his bland cubicle, hunched over his laptop that hadn't been opened or turned on. His elbows were on the desk, his fingers were in his hair, and his shoulders sagged.

"Chet, let's go get some coffee."

"I don't do coffee," Chet muttered not changing his position or posture in the least.

"Then, let's take a walk and I'll get you a Diet Coke, but I'd like to talk to you. Away from here, if that's okay."

Chet glanced up at her, stood up, brushed past her, and then stopped and said, "Sorry."

"It's okay," she said gripping his elbow lightly.

The two of them stopped at the vending machines where Summer bought Chet a Diet Coke and herself a bottle of water. Chet pushed in a couple of quarters and bought himself a Snickers.

"You want something?"

Summer smiled, and shook her head. "No thanks."

They took the elevator to the lobby and exited the building, heading to the east. There was a little outdoor café where they snagged a table and sat down.

Chet took a bite of the Snickers, washed it down with a gulp of soda, and then looked at Summer and asked, "What the hell happened in that conference room just now? What is it that Musgrave doesn't get?"

Summer sighed, took a deep breath. "You've been with the FBI for what, a year or so?"

Chet nodded.

"I've been with the agency for three years, and in that time, I've learned that the FBI is a good organization, but it is run a lot like a corporation. It's a bureaucracy with a hell of a lot of politics. You have cops… good cops, great cops, like Pete. You have really smart guys who do amazing things with a computer, like you. You have lawyers who act like cops, like me."

"You're a good cop, Summer. I've watched you and Pete. You make a great team."

Summer smiled at him. She liked Chet. She saw him as a younger brother. She, Pete and Chet were like a little one parent family.

"I'm still a lawyer, though. Probably a better lawyer than I am a cop, but I'm learning."

She took a swallow of water, and Chet took another bite of his Snickers and washed that down with another gulp of his Diet Coke. He burped quietly into the back of his hand and said, "Excuse me."

"Pete and I talked about what he was going to say when Logan asked us for a theory. Both of us knew what his reaction would be, because he's a suit. He's a good guy, but he's a suit. He and Rawson are very much aware of the politics in the FBI. Musgrave is middle management, and is supposed to keep lids on boiling pots, so to speak. And Rawson, well, because he's black. The FBI is still pretty much a good ol' boys' network, and Rawson is a minority. Don't get me wrong, Chet. Rawson is bright. He's good, but he's black. People at the top are watching him closely, so he has to watch himself or he could end up in Idaho or someplace. It's really the same for me, because I'm a woman. I have to watch what I say and do for very much the same reason as Douglas. That's the reason we couldn't take our theory to Douglas, because it would put him on a slippery slope, and he doesn't need that."

Chet nodded. "So, even though you and I agree with Pete, it was Pete's idea to give Logan the theory to protect you... us, and Rawson."

Summer smiled. "Yes. Pete figured that he's older, and he's been around longer, so he can get away with things more than you or I could."

"But Musgrave doesn't believe him. I don't get that. Pete's good. The evidence, *Jesus*, Summer, there is so much evidence to support Pete's... our theory. Why can't Logan see that?"

"Shhhh... quiet down a little," Summer said, looking around at the other tables. No one sitting close to them seemed to have heard Chet or overheard the conversation they were having.

When she was certain they could continue talking, she said, "Because, Logan has to go make a report to some suits above him. He knows they will react to him the way he reacted to Pete. The only way to get Logan and those above him to buy into our theory is to get more evidence. Once we do that, they can't deny it."

Chet stared intently at her, and then nodded. "I'll see what I can do with the computer. Tell me what I can do to help."

She smiled at him, and gripped his hand. "I will, once I know. Right now, we have three dead boys in three different states. That's not much to go on, but it's what we have to start with."

"Okay, let's do this," Chet said with a smile, "One more thing."

"What?"

"I'm a computer geek. Some might call me a computer hacker," he looked at her and smiled in a very knowing way, his eyes twinkling a little. "I don't like suits. I never have and I never will."

CHAPTER TWENTY

Fishers, Indiana

The locker room smelled of sweat and crusty four-day-old socks. Even the popular spray-on cologne couldn't cover up the smell. In fact, it only made it worse.

Brett sat on the bench in front of his locker, staring at his hands, struggling to keep his composure. His sprint coach sat next to him and waited. He had shagged the other team members out of the locker room, so he could talk to Brett alone.

"Why?" Brett asked, head still down, shoulders sagging.

Coleman shook his head. "No one knows. Police are still investigating."

"But it doesn't make any sense. I talked to him yesterday at the meet. He came over and sat down, and he talked to me like he knew me forever. He seemed..." He shook his head searching for words, "like a nice guy. He talked about how important it was for him to do well, to get good times. He said he had nothing and that he wanted to get out of here. I don't know what it meant, but he seemed like a nice guy."

"Brett, I don't know what to say."

"It's not fair."

"I know it's not. It kind of sucks."

"It's not fair," Brett said as the damn finally broke and tears fell. "I just raced him yesterday. He pushed me so hard. He pushed me harder than anyone else has this year," he said through a sob. "Why?" At that, he broke down and didn't bother to wipe his face with his shirt.

Coleman put his arm around Brett's shoulders, rested his cheek in Brett's hair, and let him cry.

They sat like that until Brett quieted down. He wiped his face off with the front of his shirt and took a deep breath.

"I need to go blow my nose," he said getting up to head to the rest room.

"You might want to splash some cold water on your face." Coleman told him.

Brett was in there for a while. Coleman heard him blow his nose and flush the toilet, and then he came out, and leaned against one of the lockers.

"Does the rest of the team know?"

Coleman shook his head. "Coach and I felt we should tell you first."

"I'd like to do something for him."

"We can send flowers to his family if you like."

Brett frowned. "I think I'd like to write to his parents. Can you get his address for me?"

"I think I can do that."

"Let's go tell the rest of the team."

Coleman stood up and held out his arms. "Come here."

Brett allowed Coleman to give him a hug, and as he still held the boy, Coleman asked, "You okay?"

"I'm okay. But it's not fair."

"I know, Brett. I know."

CHAPTER TWENTY-ONE

East of Round Rock, Navajo Indian Reservation, Arizona
It had taken George all day to gather his courage, and still, he had almost chickened out. His first attempt was after they stepped off the bus, but Rebecca ran to catch up with two of her other friends. Then, he had an opportunity later that morning between classes, but his math teacher, Eric Nobel, a *biligaana*, called him and asked him to consider taking the later bus tomorrow, so George could stay after school and review for a test.

Lunch was too crowded and too noisy. But at the end of the school day as they waited for the bus, George walked over to her, asked her to follow him, and as they stood a short distance away from their classmates who rode their same bus, he said, "I am George Tokay of the *'Azee'tsoh dine'e* and I have figured it out. I would like very much to kiss you."

Rebecca stood straight, and like a good Navajo, did not betray what she felt when she said, "I am Rebecca Morning Star of the *To'ahani* and I'll think about it." And then she walked away, leaving George staring at the place where she had once stood, not understanding, and knowing for certain that he had a lot to learn about girls.

The older kids sat in the back of the bus. George sat with Charles, towards the middle of the bus. Rebecca sat with one of her friends, towards the front. She never turned around to look at him, but George never took his eyes off her.

His stop was first, so he and his brother William got off the bus. Though he wanted to, badly, George didn't bother to look at her as he climbed down the steps. Instead, he got off the bus and walked with William, side by side, down the half-mile dirt road that led to their small ranch.

When he got home, George changed his clothes, stuffed his saddlebag with his usual supplies, and grabbed some fry bread that his mother put out for his snack. He got down on one knee and kissed his little sister Mary, who wrapped her small arms around his neck and kissed him on the cheek. "Yá'át'ééh."

George smiled at her and kissed her cheek again. He answered. "Yá'át'ééh."

He kissed his mother and his grandmother and ruffled his little brother's long black hair. "Save some lamb stew and a chunk of Mother's bread for me, okay?"

Robert looked up at him. "Okay."

George left the house, went to the barn, and saddled up the pinto. He made sure the Winchester was loaded, flicked the safety on, and shoved it into the scabbard. Then he mounted the pinto and road off to watch over the sheep.

When he was not quite to the ridge, he met his grandfather, riding down the path. They stopped and faced one another. Typically, his grandfather didn't speak much and never spoke first, so George waited patiently, as his grandfather looked at the middle afternoon sun in the sky and then at the horizon. George knew his grandfather loved this time of day, about as much as the sunrise. At this hour of the day, the desert shadows began to grow in length and paint the desert a deeper orange or pink. George loved *Diné Bikéyah*, or Navajoland, and didn't see himself ever leaving it.

"Did you have a good day, my Grandson?"

"Yes, Grandfather."

"The sheep seem restless."

George nodded.

"And your friend, the black stallion is near," his grandfather said with a sly smile. "I think he is looking for his apple and carrot, perhaps, his new friend as well."

George didn't know his grandfather knew about the wild horse and didn't know how his grandfather knew about the apple and carrot, but then again, he shouldn't have been surprised. His grandfather seemed to know everything. That is, everything that happened, and everything that was going to happen. No, George shouldn't have been surprised at all.

"Be careful out there, my Grandson," he said with a nod and perhaps a bit of a smile, though George wasn't certain about the smile. His grandfather did not show much, if any emotion. He rode his horse away towards the little ranch.

He reached the top of the ridge, tied his horse to a pine, grabbed the canteen, his saddlebag and rifle, and walked through the small stand, to the rock chair he had always used, and sat down.

The sheep grazed below them on ground that was more desert than pasture. Still, there was enough, so long as they didn't over-produce their little herd. He did a rough count and found that all sixty-four were there. He took the binoculars out of his saddlebag and searched the surrounding area for coyotes or any other predators. Nothing, just as he expected, because it was too early for predators. He knew they wouldn't appear until early evening and then long into the night.

He walked down the hillside, among the sheep, who merely gave him room to walk, but because they knew his voice and scent, they weren't afraid. He would stop and run his hand over their fluffy white coat every so often, all the while, never taking his eyes off the horizon.

His grandfather said the sheep were restless, but George didn't see anything out of the ordinary. To him, the sheep acted as they always have. They grazed quietly, contentedly. One or two would brush gently up against his pant leg. One or two others might nuzzle him gently, affectionately. But that was all, nothing out of the ordinary.

George felt the heat from the sun on his face and his bare arms. Typically, he only wore a vest, without a shirt, but he still felt the sweat run under his vest and under his hat. The distance danced in heat waves. He saw a thin rope-like trail in the sand, indicating the presence of a snake, probably a rattler. He saw rabbit tracks and what looked like coyote tracks, but those tracks seemed older. Still, he'd watch carefully.

He couldn't put a finger on it, but he had a tickle in the back of his head, which was an expression he picked up from his grandfather. The feeling wasn't big, wasn't grand, and it certainly wasn't defined. It was a feeling, or rather, a tickle, just the same. Perhaps it was his grandfather's comment that the sheep seemed restless, perhaps. To be safe, he flicked the safety off his Winchester .22 and had it ready.

CHAPTER TWENTY-TWO

Washington, D.C.

It was evening and by anyone's standards, she should have been calling it a day. But with three dead boys and no leads, Summer and her team had been working almost nonstop. She passed up getting a bite to eat with Pete and Chet, because she had an unexpected appointment.

Summer rarely ventured anywhere near the top floors of the Hoover Building, so when she received the call that Thatcher Davis wanted to see her, she was curious. She did a quick search and found out he was a lawyer, and in charge of the legal division that advised the director and deputy directors on any issues that might hit the newspapers or the six o'clock news. The legal division was responsible for making sure the agents and the agency remained aboveboard, honest, and squeaky clean, at least, visible to the public. That made Summer more than curious, because there was nothing her team had done that would have crossed any lines.

She stepped out of the elevator, walked down the hall, and entered a corner office suite. The reception area was larger than the standard she was used to on the first and second floors, and she surmised that it was good to be towards the top of the food chain.

"It's late and I'm just about to close up, but may I help you?" The pleasant, older receptionist asked.

"Yes, I have an appointment with Thatcher Davis."

"Oh, you're Agent Storm. I'll let Mr. Davis know you've arrived."

Interesting, the receptionist referred to him as Mister, instead of Agent, Summer thought.

She continued to stand and wait. She didn't know why she was here, and she wanted to get back to work on the kids. Luckily, she didn't have to wait long.

"Summer Storm?"

She turned towards the door and saw Davis. Tall, slender, older than she thought he might be, and the kind of man that seemed to have money, and a touch of elegance. They shook hands and his grip was light and rather weak, but his face and smile were kind.

"Yes, Sir."

"Thatcher or Thatch, please," he said kindly, as he ushered her into his office, closing the door behind them. He showed her to a leather chair, facing a desk of dark wood, probably a faux mahogany, but she could be wrong. She didn't think the FBI would pop for something expensive unless one was at the top of the food chain, and she doubted that Davis was that high up.

"How can I help you, Mr. Davis?" Summer asked.

He sat behind his desk and opened up a file, presumably hers, she thought. He smiled at her. "Thatcher, please. And, it's not what you can do for me, really. It's what I think I can do for you."

She blinked, not expecting that from him.

He picked up some paperwork from the folder. "You graduated near the top of your class at Louisville... Law school."

Summer nodded.

"I have an opening in my division for a good legal mind. I'm going to retire in three years, perhaps five, and you have an excellent track record. Your service evaluations have been perfect. You have a wonderful reputation as a leader, and more importantly, you're a lawyer."

When Summer entered into the FBI, she purposely chose the Crimes Against Children Unit, because she wanted cop work, though she didn't consider herself to be much of a cop. At least she didn't see herself as in the same class as Pete. But she wanted Kiddie Corps, because she wanted to make a difference, a real difference. She wanted to do something that mattered—at least to her.

"I enjoy the unit I'm with, Sir, but I appreciate the offer."

Davis closed the file and folded his manicured hands on top of it. The way he sat, the way he shook her hand, she wondered if he was gay. Not that she had anything against anyone being gay, especially since one of the FBI legends had J. Edgar Hoover, himself, as being gay, and even a closet cross-dresser. It was a thought that crossed her mind, though. At the very least, Davis had a good dose of effeminate stuffed inside that hand-tailored gray suit.

"I ask that you don't take me wrong, but I'd like to ask a question or two."

Summer nodded.

"How many cases have you closed since you joined The Crimes Against Children Unit, Agent Storm?"

She shifted uncomfortably, and set her jaw. "Not as many as I would have liked, but we have closed some cases."

"Please, Summer... may I call you, Summer?" Not waiting for a response, he went on and said, "I'm not judging you or your team at all. Not in the least. What you people do is admirable. It's tough, difficult work. So many children harmed and in harm's way. Any reasonable person would not expect you and your team to bring home all of the missing the kids, alive."

Storm sat still. She didn't like being patronized and it felt like she was being patronized—by a suit, no less. At the least Davis seemed condescending.

"You have a fine mind and I would like to put that fine mind to good use."

"Thank you, Sir, but I believe I'm putting my mind to good use."

Davis frowned, made a tsk, tsk noise. "I don't mean to imply that you aren't."

Summer folded her arms and stared at the man.

He seemed to think twice about what he was going to say next, started once and stopped, and then said, "Your partner, Pete Kelliher . . . he's not particularly well thought of. There are those who feel he's a loose cannon, sort of a holdover from a bygone era."

"He's an experienced veteran and a great cop. Better than most, far better."

Davis smiled, but sincerity never touched his eyes. "I appreciate the fact that you support him, as well you should, because he's a member of your team. I merely point out that there are those above you and me who don't see him that way. They see him as being on the downside of his career. I, and some others who shall remain nameless, don't want to see him take you down with him."

Summer stood up. "I appreciate the offer *Mister* Davis," emphasizing the *Mister*, "but I can watch out for myself and frankly, I don't care what suits think about my partner, who I feel is a valuable member of my team, and who also, happens to be my mentor and my friend."

Davis stood and put his hands up. "Agent Storm, I surrender. I did my research and found a wonderful agent who would be a great addition and an eventual leader in my division. There are others who think so too."

"Thank you for the visit. Again, I appreciate the offer."

"Please, before you leave," he said walking around the desk. "Here is my card. My cell and home numbers are on the back. If at any time you'd like to talk, I want you to know I'd be happy to listen. If there is some difficult road that leads to a question, perhaps anything legal or otherwise that you'd like to bounce off an independent mind, someone who is objective, and not in your inner circle,

I want you to know I'm willing to be there for you. There are some in this organization who feel I am a good mentor and friend, too."

Summer took the card. "Thank you," she shook his weak hand and left the office shoving his card in the breast pocket of her blazer. Maybe, she thought, he was trying to be friendly and sincere, but was just too socially inept to pull it off.

However, she left the reception area without even so much as a look back, and decided to take the stairs that were near the elevators, because she wanted to work off some of the anger she felt. She also wanted to regain her composure, before she bumped into anyone on her team or anyone else, for that matter, for fear of ripping someone's head off.

CHAPTER TWENTY-THREE

East of Round Rock, Navajo Indian Reservation, Arizona

The black stallion appeared on the ridge, above the small pasture, where the sheep grazed. George thought it was deciding if it was safe to advance, or more likely, it was waiting for George to bring his daily dessert of an apple and a carrot.

George sat in his rocking chair, in the shadow of the pines, watching over the sheep and searching the horizon, staring long and hard at the growing shadows as the sun hung just above the horizon. To be honest, he had hoped Rebecca showed up, but so far, she hadn't come around, and he had all but given up hope of her coming. He was disappointed, and if he was honest with himself, maybe even a little hurt. But it also confirmed to him for the second time that day that he had a lot to learn about girls.

With a sigh and resignation, he dug the apple and carrot out of the saddlebag and started up towards the stallion. About half-way there, he remembered the binoculars and rifle, but because it had been a quiet day, and because it was almost time to bring the sheep in for the night, he decided he would be alright without them.

As he neared the horse, he slowed his approach, because he didn't want to spook it. He began talking quietly, soothingly, holding the apple out in front of him.

"I brought you your apple. Are you hungry?"

The horse stomped its front hoof and shook its head, shaking its thick mane, swooshing its long black tail.

"If you want it, you have to come get it this time," George said confidently.

The black stallion reared up, took a few steps in one direction, and then the other, backing up, coming forward, and whinnying loudly with each step. It seemed to George that the horse glared at him.

But George was more than patient and he could also be stubborn, so he waited a long time as the stallion protested. It would trot away only to trot back. It would shake its great black head and swish its tail, and paw the ground. And all the while, George stood there with the apple in his hand, arm outstretched, talking quietly and soothingly.

And at last, he was rewarded as the horse stepped up tentatively, cautiously, and sniffed George, then the apple, and then took the apple from George, munching it in greedy fashion.

The horse finished with the apple, so George reached into his vest pocket slowly without ever taking his eyes off the horse that seemed to be eyeing him with suspicion. Like he did with the apple, he held the carrot out in front of him and this time, without any protest or hesitation, the stallion took the carrot from George's hand and ate it, and then stood in front of George waiting.

Waiting for what? George wondered.

On a gamble and a hunch, George reached out his empty hand and stroked the stallion's cheek, carefully keeping his hand away from the horse's mouth. In response, the horse grunted, snorted softly, and nudged George's stomach with its nose.

Stepping slowly and cautiously, George moved to the side so he could stroke and pet the horse's neck and back. The stallion merely looked over its shoulder at George, and then back out over the pasture at the sheep.

George stroked the horse, but never ventured past the horse's flank, and slowly made his way back to the stallion's head, continuing to pet and pat and stroke the horse, talking softly and gently.

And that was when George heard the truck's engine and saw the dust cloud it had created. The sheep moved away from it and further up into the pasture. George stood next to the horse and watched as it backed up the trailer onto the Tokay land. Never having seen the truck or trailer before, he knew who they were and what they had wanted.

Forgetting the stallion, he ran along the upper end of the ridge, taking the long way back to his stand. He picked up his rifle, angry with himself for not having it with him. He ran through the pines to his Pinto, mounted it, and rode it through the pines and down into the pasture towards the truck.

He saw two men, one young, one old, either Mexican or perhaps Apache, but he knew they weren't Navajo or Ute, because he didn't recognize either of them. He did read the Arizona plate and memorize the license, as well as the coloring of the truck and the clothes the two men wore.

"What are you doing on our land?" George said as bravely as a mature fifth grader could sound.

The older man spat tobacco juice, took off his hat, scratched his greasy long black hair, and replaced the hat back on his head.

"We figured we would make your babysittin' easier by taken' a couple sheep off your hands," he said with a laugh.

"They are not for sale."

"Who said anything about buying 'em?" The young one said with a smile, but without any humor.

"You are not welcome on our land and you may not take our sheep."

"You go on back to wherever you was, Kid, and leave us be now," the older one said. "We be gone real quick."

The younger one stepped towards George and that was when the first shot rang out, the bullet spitting up red clay inches from the man's foot.

The second shot punctured the rear trailer tire on the side closest to the ridge.

"Shit! Who the fuck is up there, Kid?"

George struggled to keep the smile off his face because he knew who it was.

And for the second surprise of the night, the big, black stallion quietly appeared next to George and pawed the ground.

A third shot rang out, flattening the front tire making one side of the large cattle trailer less mobile and tilted.

Loudly and clearly, George said, "You should leave now, before my friend starts on your truck."

"*Bendejo!*" The young one shouted as he advanced. But George moved his Pinto backwards out of his reach and out of the way.

The Stallion stepped forward and reared up on its hind legs and landed almost on top of the young man, stopping the young man in his tracks.

He back-peddled quickly.

"Let's go," the old man said.

"You little fucker! *Tu madre' es puta!*" the young man said.

The Stallion apparently heard and saw enough and charged at the young man, knocking him back, sending him in an ass over his head summersault, and then stood over him, its powerful black legs and deadly hooves so near the man's head.

"Get up slowly, get in your truck, and leave," George said, not sure what the Stallion would do next.

The man slowly got up on his hands and knees and then just as slowly to his feet, climbed into the truck with the older man and they drove away, dragging the lopsided trailer behind them.

George sat on his pinto, his rifle at the ready, and watched them leave. Only when they disappeared down the dirt road did he breathe a sigh of relief. And it was only then that he heard the horse come up behind him.

"A good Navajo doesn't sneak up on someone without a greeting. And a good Navajo doesn't make that much noise," George teased. He never turned around.

"A good Navajo wouldn't have relied on someone to cover his back, and a good Navajo wouldn't rely on a wild horse to come to his aid."

Rebecca rode up next to him. George noticed that the Winchester .44 was at the ready and he said, "I knew it was you."

"How?"

He smiled at her. "You're a better shot than Charles, more patient."

She leaned around him and stared at the black stallion as it pawed the ground.

"What did you name him?"

George had been considering names, but didn't know if it was the right time or if it was even the proper thing to do. Technically, the stallion was wild and of the desert, so it belonged to no man. Still, it seemed that the stallion and George were becoming friends and the stallion did defend George against the younger of the two men. The stallion hadn't moved away, but in fact stood right next to George and the pinto, actually up against George's leg. He didn't shy away when Rebecca approached, though he did eye Rebecca suspiciously.

George reached over and stroked the big horse's neck and said, "I am not sure yet. I want to wait and see."

CHAPTER TWENTY-FOUR

Fishers, Indiana

Brett had been restless all day long, the same as he was the day before. He was unable to concentrate in school, unable to take part in the jokes that he normally laughed at or participated in between classes, or in the cafeteria. At track practice, he pushed and punished himself, thrashing everyone he ran against. He outran, out jumped, and out hustled everyone. He wouldn't stop. He couldn't stop. He dared not stop.

Brett couldn't get Da'Shawn Grimes out of his head. He couldn't comprehend the meaningless, senseless death made all the more tragic, because apparently, he was yards away from his front steps, his porch and his family. It made no sense, none. A kid who had a dream of going to college, of getting away from... *what?* Brett didn't know, other than that Grimes saw that he might have a way out through track or football, or both, and now? Now he was dead, a thirteen-year-old kid. He kept coming back to it not being fair.

He would replay the track meet over and over in school, at home when he was supposed to be doing his homework or eating dinner, and as he lay awake in bed at night. One minute talking to him, the next minute, racing against him. And when it was all done and over with, the same finality, the same result. Grimes was dead.

How can that possibly happen?

As Brett walked the track alone, Austin Hemple jogged up to him. "You okay?"

Brett glared at him, turned, and walked away.

Hemple grabbed his arm to stop him, and Brett turned around, placed both hands on his chest and shoved him backwards. Hemple landed on his butt, but Brett turned around and stormed off, leaving Hemple on the ground, staring after him.

Coach Coleman saw what had happened and followed Brett onto the grass infield and sat down on the grass next to him.

"Talk to me."

Brett shook his head, drew his knees up to this chest and hugged them tightly, keeping his eyes downcast.

Coleman waited patiently, searching for the right words, but coming up empty.

"I just... I can't..." and Brett gave up trying.

Coleman looked around to make sure no one was close by and when he saw that they were alone, he said, "Brett, I don't have any answers for you. I can't explain why it happened. I can't. The only thing I can say is that sometimes shit happens. It's not fair. There isn't a rhyme or a reason for it, but sometimes shit happens."

Brett didn't raise his eyes.

"At some point, Brett, you have to let it go and move on."

Brett lifted his head slowly, his eyes glistening with tears. "And how do you think I should do that?"

"Do you think that young man, Da'Shawn Grimes, would want you moping around, pushing around your best friend, and sulking? You've not been yourself for two days, ever since that boy was murdered, and you've got to pull yourself together. Look around you. The kids on this team look up to you. Yes, you're only a fifth grader and there are other older kids on this team, but you're their leader. They take their cue from you, no one else."

Brett glared at him, but he dissolved in tears. He didn't know why Grimes' death affected him so much. He didn't know him. Brett couldn't name the kid's favorite food or his favorite football team. He didn't know anything about him, but the thought of Grimes walking home from a track meet, and then laying on the sidewalk in front of his house, dead with a bullet in his face and several to his chest, was something Brett couldn't comprehend. He couldn't wrap his mind around it.

Much like he did in the locker room when he first told, Coleman got up and then sat down next to Brett and put his arm around his shoulders.

"Kid, you have to pull yourself together. Grimes was a tough kid. He was a great athlete. But I think he'd want you to go on living your life. He'd want you to race. He'd want you to do well in school. He'd want you to be a leader. That's the best way to remember him, to keep his memory alive."

Brett felt so small. He didn't feel like a leader. He didn't know what he wanted or what he needed, but deep down on some level, Brett knew Coach Coleman was right. But he also knew he wouldn't let Da'Shawn Grimes' memory die along with the boy. He wouldn't let that happen.

CHAPTER TWENTY-FIVE

Indianapolis, Indiana

He had no idea that the death of Grimes would make that much difference to Brett. In fact, he thought it would be just the opposite—that Brett would be happy, ecstatic because he was now the fastest kid in Indiana, and one of the fastest middle school kids in the nation. And he wasn't even in middle school yet, at least technically, not until September.

Maybe he should help Brett man up some. Maybe a little light stuff now, heavier stuff later, maybe. He'd have to think about that. He knew the time was coming when he and Brett would have a relationship. A real relationship. He was working on Brett some, and he knew he needed to increase it. He knew he needed to pick up the pace. Not too much though, because he didn't want to alarm him or his family.

As for the Grimes kid, in time, Brett would forget about him. In time, Brett would understand the gift that had been given to him. In time, Brett would appreciate him, and love him.

He had always hated Brett's parents, Thomas and Victoria. He couldn't stand them. He knew he would be much better for Brett and his brother, Bobby, than Thomas or Victoria ever would or could be.

Thomas, the university professor, a nerd. The English teacher, who wrote two meaningless, boring books and who thought he was an intellectual, and smarter than everyone else. How in the hell he ever got it raised long and hard enough to have two kids, two beautiful and handsome boys, he didn't know. Sheer luck, he imagined.

Victoria, the simpleton, A nurse, who fussed and bothered and slaved over other simpletons. Victoria, plain and ordinary, who lacked any imagination at all. *How could she have given birth to two handsome, beautiful boys?* Boys who were strong and smart. *How was it possible that those two boys could have her blood in their veins?*

In time, when he was ready for Brett, and when Brett was ready for him, then he might take care of good old Thomas and Victoria, once and for all. He'd have to figure out what to do with Bobby. Two might be difficult. Fun, but difficult. He would have to see.

But sooner or later, he'd have Brett. Probably sooner rather than later. Real soon.

CHAPTER TWENTY-SIX

Washington, D.C.

Chet had gone through two keyboards on his desktop computer already, and the third was wearing out. Fueled on nothing but Mt. Dew and Snickers, and operating on less than seven hours sleep in the last forty-eight hours, his nerves were frayed and he was crashing fast. He was also sick and disgusted from what he had been viewing and researching, and he knew as long as he lived, he'd never get the pictures or the sounds out of his head. Not ever.

He grabbed the desk phone off the cradle, punched in an extension and waited as it buzzed. When she answered, he said, "Summer, can you and Pete meet me in the conference room? I have something to show you."

Summer and Pete hoped it would be good news, and some kind of lead, because for the past few days, and ever since finding the Monroe boy in Michigan, they were in a holding pattern with nothing to go on, with no one to look for, and no leads whatsoever. And worse, both Pete and Summer knew they were waiting for the next body to show up and only the good Lord knew when that would happen and where it would be found this time.

They entered the room and found Chet by himself, with his laptop, a half-can of Dew, and a quarter of a Snickers on the table, and Chet holding his head in his hands with his eyes shut.

"Chet, you look awful. When was the last time you slept?" Summer said.

He shook his head. "We don't have time for that."

Summer sighed. "Chet, you aren't going to be any help to us if you get sick."

"I've been online and on the phone with the cyber guys in Quantico, and I've been looking at some really ugly shit," he stopped and shook his head. "Guys, look at this."

Summer and Pete sat down on either side of him, close enough to see the screen clearly. Chet keyed in a website and then sat back far enough to let them see for themselves.

Appearing on the screen were titles of internet HTML links to various porn websites, all featuring young boys and girls. Chet clicked one and appearing on the screen were naked boys performing sex acts with each other, or by themselves. All were the same, yet different. One picture after another.

Chet clicked on a picture of a blond boy and a brown haired boy, both appearing to be eleven- or twelve-years-old. That picture led to ten other pictures. He clicked on one of them, and that picture led to ten more, including videos. Each website invited the viewer to register for even better pictures and videos.

"I thought child pornography was against the law," Pete said quietly.

"It is," Chet answered. "The cyber guys told me they can shut down one website, but then three more will pop up. They said it's like a game of Whack A Mole, but it's no fucking game. It's kids," Chet said rubbing his eyes.

"They ran a sting and shut down a ring in Mississippi and Louisiana, where kids nine through fifteen were coerced into snap-chatting and posting selfies online, and then they were blackmailed into performing sex acts on themselves or with others while it was recorded and posted online. The perverts who ran the ring hosted a closed internet site for subscribers. One of the cyber guys posed as a pervert who was interested in this kind of crap. In the end, nineteen boys were freed, and four or five assholes from Alabama to Louisiana were arrested."

"Well, that's something," Summer said.

"Yeah," Chet nodded. "True. But then, more of this shit shows up with other kids, and you know damn well they aren't running this shit by themselves. Some pervert is behind it. Probably more than one asshole."

He closed down that site and clicked on another, and another. And then another.

"Guys, I can do this all day and all night long. This is all I've been doing for two days, website after website. They're all the same, all of them. Little kids, kids in middle school, kids in high school, older kids, kids with adults, boys, girls. Kids from the US and kids from other countries," he stopped and shook his head. "It's sick, and I don't understand it. I just don't get it," he said shaking his head. "It's sick. It's wrong, just wrong."

Pete sat back in his chair. "By chance, did you see any of our three kids in any of that stuff?"

Chet shook his head. "The cyber guys ran facial recognition software and came up with zip. The problem is, we can sit in front of a computer and watch this crap all day, and I don't know if we'd ever find them, because there's too much of it to go through."

Summer saw Chet's hands were shaking as he lifted them to his face, his fingers in his hair. She put a hand on his shoulder and gave it a gentle squeeze. "Calm down, Chet."

He looked up at her. "Calm down, *really?* How can I calm down, Summer?"

Pete lost count of the number of sites they viewed and the number of kids in the pictures. At some point, Summer turned her head and stared at the wall with the pictures of the three boys they had found. The team put up the missing posters of the three boys, along with their names, the city and state they were from, their birthdates and ages, and lastly, a picture of the boys as they were found dead, along with the date and their age at death. It was a gruesome shrine, but a necessary one just the same. It was evidence, and hopefully, it would lead to a clue, a connection to help end it all.

"I've only been in the FBI for a year or so, but how do you two do this shit? How can you stand to see these kids used like this? How do you do this?" Chet said almost in a whisper. "How is it possible that some perverts are so fucked up they can use, hurt and kill kids like this? How?"

Chet was pale and sweating and had dark circles under his eyes. He was so pale, his red hair and his freckles stood out more prominently than they normally did.

"How do you explain this shit? How do you do this?"

"Chet, turn this off, okay?" Pete said as he pushed his chair away from the table and stared at the wall with the three boys' pictures and information. Still facing the wall, he said, "You focus on the kids we save. You focus on putting one pervert away and then another. That's how Summer and I do what we do. You have to focus on one kid, one family at a time."

That was the only answer he had for Chet, and he knew it wasn't nearly good enough, but he knew Summer felt the same way.

More importantly, he knew they needed to find the perverts responsible for killing these kids, and that they needed to find the perverts soon. However, he knew deep down, as did Summer, and even on some level even Chet knew, that there would be more bodies, more dead boys before this was over.

CHAPTER TWENTY-SEVEN

East of Round Rock, Navajo Indian Reservation, Arizona
"George, I have to go pee."

Robert was only five and slept in the middle between George and William, in the full-sized bed. He wore a smile, his hair long like George and William, and he looked more like his father than George or William did. But like George and William, Robert was a handsome boy.

It didn't happen often, but every now and then, Robert would wake up George in the middle of the night to take him to the outhouse.

George swung his legs over the side of the bed and slipped into his moccasins. Then Robert climbed onto his back and he walked silently through the dark house, and out the door, shutting it quietly behind them.

The outhouse was a short distance from the house, and near the corral that held the horses. When they reached it, he set Robert down. "Hurry, okay?"

Robert nodded, went inside and a little later, came out. George bent down, so Robert, who was barefoot, could climb onto his back for the short trip back to the house.

When they reached the front steps, however, Robert said, "George, can we watch the stars?"

George sighed, but this was part of the ritual that went with Robert needing to go to the bathroom at night, so he set Robert down on the top step and then sat down next to him. Instead, Robert climbed onto George's lap.

"I like that one," Robert whispered, pointing to a bright star near the moon. It was always the same star each night they went out. It never varied.

"I think that's Venus. It's a planet."

"It's a big one," Robert answered breathlessly.

He slipped his arm around George's neck and held him tightly.

"Why do you like stars?"

Robert turned to him, eyes wide and a beautiful smile. "Because, they're up there, and they don't fall down."

George chuckled, and Robert kissed his cheek, and together, they looked at the stars some more.

"Show me the North Star," George said.

Robert stood up, had one hand on George's shoulder for balance as he turned one way and then the other, searching for the dipper.

"There!" Robert said in little more than a whisper.

"And what does it do?"

Robert stared at the star, his face screwed down in concentration, and then his eyes widened and a smile broke over his face. "It tells you what direction North is!"

"That's your marker in case you're ever lost," George said.

George heard it first and looked off into the darkness.

"What's that?" Robert whispered; a little frightened.

George stood up slowly and placed his hand on Robert's shoulder, pushing him a little behind him.

The black stallion appeared out of the darkness, stood and stared at them, its black tail, swishing back and forth.

"Where did it come from?" Robert asked in a whisper.

"Out there somewhere, from the night."

"Whose horse is that?"

"I don't know... no ones," George answered never taking his eyes from the stallion.

George approached, slowly and cautiously. "What are you doing here, Boy? Hmmm? Are you lost?"

Robert appeared at George's side and held onto George's arm, but otherwise, didn't say anything or make a noise.

"Stay here, Robert," George said as he walked slowly towards the horse.

He reached the horse and stroked his neck, the area between the eyes, and then its side and back. When he looked back, he saw Robert petting the horse's chest and the stallion let him.

"Is he your horse, George?"

"I don't know. I think we're just friends."

"I think he likes you. I think he likes me, too."

Robert stepped to the side and tried to pet the stallion's back, but only reached up to his belly. He tried to go further, but George stopped him.

"Don't go anywhere near the back of any horse, Robert. They might hurt you, even though they don't mean to. Promise me, okay?"

"Okay, George. I promise."

"I think it's time for bed. I have to get up early for school."

Robert hugged the stallion's chest. "Goodnight, horse. Come back and visit soon, okay?" Then he turned to George. "What's his name?"

George thought for a minute, "Nochero."

"Nochero? I like that name. What's it mean?"

"It's Spanish, for *'protector of the night'*."

"Oh," Robert said, his eyes large, "Nochero is our protector?"

George glanced at him and then back towards the horse. "He is one of our protectors, I think."

They walked back into the house and George stopped and gave the stallion one last look. The stallion swished its tail, snorted softly, turned and left as silently as it came.

The two boys climbed back into bed carefully, so as to not wake up William, who didn't even stir on his side of the bed.

Before they shut their eyes, Robert gave George a kiss on the cheek and then curled against him, resting his head on George's arm. George held Robert in his arms and it didn't take long for Robert to fall back asleep. It never did.

George shut his eyes, but remained awake. Instead, he considered the wild stallion and why the two of them had become friends. He was content with the fact that Nochero was out there somewhere, close by, watching over him and his family, protecting them.

CHAPTER TWENTY-EIGHT

Washington, D.C.

As far as rivers went, the Muskingum River in Ohio meandered mostly east and west, but there was a smallish section that bent north and south in what looked like a big bulge in an artery about to burst in an aneurysm. The river was long, and mostly ran in the middle of nowhere. And it was in the middle of nowhere, near that big bulge, and near the small town of Coal Run that a party of six, traveling in canoes, found the body of Gary Haynes, a fourteen-year-old, from Lansing, Michigan. He had been missing for two years.

Because he was found on the banks of the river, identifying him was difficult, due to advanced decomposition, and the fact that critters had been feasting for some time on his soft tissue. But DNA and dental records helped identify the boy, and the body wasn't so decomposed that they couldn't see the remnants of whip marks, and the telltale sign of the upside-down cross on the left ankle. The ME confirmed cause of death was two shots to the back of the head, from a small caliber weapon, most likely a .38, just like the other three boys that had been previously found. And to top it off, just like the other three boys, he was naked and his hands were bound behind his back with handcuffs.

Summer was not only sad, she was angry and frustrated.

Four bodies, in four states, in no distinguishable pattern other than the remoteness of the areas in which the bodies were found.

She pushed her chair back from her desk, bent over it with her palms flat on the surface as she studied the pictures of the Haynes boy, and then stood up, stretched, and ran her hands through her short blond hair. She had been trying to put together a report for the team and Musgrave, but so far, it read just like the previous three. No stunning revelations. No conclusions, nothing that would contribute to a theory.

She grabbed her cell from her otherwise neat and tidy desk, and punched in Pete's number. "I'm done, but I don't have anything. It's just a bunch of words on paper."

Pete, who was in the conference room, ran a hand over his face. He pushed up from the table where he had been sitting, reading and rereading his ever-present little notebook. He stepped over to the whiteboard that had the pictures of the boys. Chet was hunched over his laptop, but every so often, he checked in with the cyber guys at Quantico.

"Summer, I don't know what to tell you. Chet has been working nonstop with Quantico chasing some kind of thread, but I don't know if it will lead to anything."

"What thread?"

Pete shook his head. "He didn't say, and I didn't push, because you know him. Once he gets in that zone…"

Summer knew what he meant by the zone. When Chet chased something, he drew within, clammed up and did nothing but peck away on his laptop or computer, so it was best to leave him alone.

"When do we bring the team together?"

Pete shook his head. "Let's wait until the weekly briefing. If Logan gives you any grief, tell him it was my idea. Blame it on me."

Chet stopped typing and looked up. "Pete, put her on speaker."

A bit puzzled, Pete looked at him for a moment, but then did as he was told and put the cell on the table between them.

"Summer, I don't like it that Pete's taking all the heat on this."

"Chet…" Pete said tiredly.

"No, it's bullshit. You don't have to cover for me."

"Chet, listen," Pete said, hands up trying to calm him down. "Please, listen."

"He's right, Pete. I'm a big girl. I can take care of myself."

"Both of you, just shut up and stop, alright. Just listen a minute."

Chet glared at him and Pete imagined Summer was glaring at a wall or something, pretending it was Pete.

"I'm what, five or so years from retirement? I could go now and be very comfortable, but you two have long careers that you have to consider. Guys, both of you know that this place can get claustrophobic with all the rules, regulations, and political bullshit. You both know that. The FBI likes things nice, neat and tidy. They don't like loose ends, and they don't want to deal with anything messy and ugly. And they sure as hell don't want to deal with anything that has few, if any, answers."

"Pete, do you know how much money I can make in the real world? I don't need the FBI," Chet said.

"Chet, you won't get anywhere with anyone if you get black-balled or canned by the FBI."

"It could actually make me more marketable in the right sector."

"And I can always do the lawyer thing," Summer chimed in.

"Yes, but where else can you get minimum pay, crappy hours, and a shitty office?" Pete said with a laugh.

The three of them laughed and then Pete said, "I just need you two to hold off a little bit longer. Let me take the heat a little while longer, just until we have something, something substantial. Okay?"

"Why? Why should you take the shit and we can't?" Chet asked.

Pete smiled. "Because, I have something neither of you two have."

"Besides a cheap haircut and off the rack sport coats, what do you have?" Summer asked.

"A guardian angel," Pete said with a wink at Chet.

CHAPTER TWENTY-NINE

Fishers, Indiana
It rained steadily all day. No thunder or lightning, but a nice, steady, Midwestern rain that was good for the crops, for newly planted flowers, and for recently fertilized lawns. Because of the rain, track practice was canceled, so Brett got a ride home from Austin's mom after school, leaving his brother Bobby to walk home with a couple of his friends.

Even though Austin's mom drove excruciatingly slow, Brett got home before Bobby did. He punched in the garage code and then pushed the button to shut the garage door, before opening up the door to the mudroom, which was actually part of the laundry room. He slipped off his shoes, which was a rule in the house, and walked into the kitchen.

Like always, he slipped out of his backpack, dropped it in the doorway that led to the family room and the hallway to the bedrooms. He went to the refrigerator and pulled out a gallon of milk. He found a glass in the cupboard and poured himself a glass. He drank half of it while still holding the gallon of milk, and then refilled his glass and put the gallon away. Brett sat down at the table and found the note left by his mother that morning, before she left for the hospital. He read it as he absentmindedly wiped the remnants of a milk mustache off his mouth with the back of his hand.

Victoria had to work three heart surgeries that day, so she'd be home late. Thomas had an evening lecture, so he'd be home even later. Mac n' Cheese was in the pantry for dinner, and there were brownies in the pan on the counter for dessert, and the inevitable reminder to get all of their homework done.

Bobby could make dinner, Brett decided.

He went back to the refrigerator, pulled open a drawer and grabbed an orange, shut the refrigerator and walked over to the sink and peeled it, and then ran the sink disposal while running water from the faucet to get rid of the rinds. He sat back down at the table and ate it slice by slice.

The only homework he had was to write a poem for language arts. He hated poetry. He liked and excelled at both math and science. He even liked social studies some, but he hated English, even if his dad was an English professor at

Butler University. And, even though he pulled a low B in it, he hated it, especially poetry.

He finished with the orange and his milk, went to the sink, rinsed out the glass and put it in the dishwasher, and then washed and dried his hands. He looked out the window towards the street. It was still drizzling, but it seemed to lighten up some.

Brett walked through the kitchen and snagged his backpack on the way to his bedroom.

He opened up the door, stepped inside, walked over to his desk and set the backpack down next to it. Then, he flopped down on his soft queen-sized bed on his back with his hands folded behind his head and stared at the ceiling, and yawned.

While he was tired, he wasn't in the mood for a nap. What he wanted to do was go for a run. The rain would feel good.

He rolled over and placed his stocking feet on the carpeted floor, and pulled off the polo shirt he wore.

And that's when he noticed it.

Brett was a kind of neat freak. Nothing like the neat freak Bobby was, but a neat freak just the same.

The top drawer was open just a little. So was the closet door.

Brett knew he never left a drawer open, and an open closet door freaked him out, especially at night.

He stood up and looked back at his bed.

Brett made his bed every morning before going to the kitchen for breakfast. It wasn't made as neatly as he had made it, and it wasn't because he had just gotten up from it.

He dropped his shirt on the foot of the bed, unsure of what to do next.

Did Bobby go into his room before they left for school? No, they left together and Bobby was already in the kitchen, eating breakfast when Brett got there. *Did his mom or dad go into his room?* He doubted it, because his father seldom came into his room, and his mother only to bring in cleaned clothes. And then, she would place them on his bed for him to put away.

Brett stepped over to his dresser and pulled the top drawer open.

His boxers had been moved slightly.

He stepped over to the closet and hesitated, wondering if someone was still in there. He flung it open, but found no one. But a pair of jeans was off the hanger, on the floor, on top of his shoes. *Had they fallen somehow?*

He picked up the jeans, rehung them, picked up the polo shirt he had just taken off and went to his laundry basket. That was when he knew for certain someone had been in his room.

The clothes he had on yesterday weren't on the top of the dirty clothes, like they should have been. Instead, there was a pair of boxers and a sock. He remembered burying the sock and the boxers deep down among the dirty clothes, because they had been wet and sticky with his semen from the other night, and Brett didn't want his mom to find it. But there, right on top of the pile, was the sock and the boxers. No longer were they wet and sticky, but stiff and crusty, and embarrassing for Brett, because someone found them.

Why? That was one question, and he didn't have an answer for it. More urgently was *who?*

Brett was certain someone had been in his room. What he didn't know was if that someone was still in the house.

CHAPTER THIRTY

Fishers, Indiana
Generally, Brett wasn't afraid of much of anything. He was confident, but not cocky. He was smart, but not in a nerdy sort of way. More than most kids, he had a lot of qualities going for him. But this time, he didn't know what to do next.

Brett turned around slowly to face the door, wondering if somebody was still in the house, and if that somebody might be standing there.

The doorway was empty.

On his tip-toes, he stepped out into the hallway.

Bobby's door was closed. *Should he go in there?*

He never really went into Bobby's room. He and his brother got along, but they didn't have much to do with one another. Bobby was into computers, and books, and music and the piano. Brett was all about sports and recently, girls. *But if he did go into Bobby's room, what if someone was in there?*

He stepped quietly over to Bobby's door and listened.

Nothing.

As fast as he could, he turned the doorknob and threw the door open and rushed inside.

No one.

His closet door was shut tight, as was his dresser drawers. So were his windows.

Brett didn't check the windows in his bedroom, so he tiptoed back to his room and saw that his windows were shut also.

So, how did someone get into the house?

Brett stuck his head into his parents' room and it looked like everything was where it should be. Everything closed. Bed made. Windows shut. He went into the master bath. Nothing, and no one.

He walked back into the hallway and stuck his head into the bathroom he and Bobby shared. The shower had a frosted glass door, no curtain, so no one was hiding in the tub.

He shut that door, along with Bobby's and his own, and stood in the hallway.

There was the study, the family room, the living room, the kitchen, and the basement. He didn't want to go down into the basement by himself, so he'd wait until Bobby got home.

Brett tiptoed to the study. The door was always open, so he wasn't surprised that it was open now. Only one closet, so Brett boldly walked over to it, jerked it open, and found nothing but a clutter of files and boxes, and papers that he supposed were in some kind of order, at least to his dad and mom.

He went to the family room. Nothing out of place, one closet. He walked over to it and opened both doors at once. No one, just board games, Wii games and other game kind of stuff, but no one. He shut both doors and turned to the sliding glass door.

Unlocked.

And it was never unlocked during the day, never. Not only unlocked, but it was slightly open. Not a lot, but more than a little.

Brett felt a sudden chill. The hair on the back of his neck stood at attention and he had a queasy feeling in the pit of his stomach.

Why would someone dig through his dresser drawer and his dirty laundry? What did they want?

CHAPTER THIRTY-ONE

Fishers, Indiana

Lucky. Very lucky, almost got caught, but almost doesn't count for anything except horseshoes and hand grenades.

Fortunately, when Brett turned on the sink disposal, it covered any noise that he might have made as he quick-walked from Brett's bedroom, into the family room, and out the sliding glass door. He hesitated long enough to determine that no one was outside watching as he hopped the small fence, crossed a neighbor's backyard and got to his car that was parked three doors down from the McGovern house.

The quick foray into Brett's room excited him. He always got a kick out of a B and E. He had always found it exhilarating, even better if there was a little bodily harm involved. That really jacked him up. However, none was necessary on this little trip. He thought about taking the sock and the boxers with him, but counted on the fact that Brett was a smart boy. A very smart boy, who would know someone had been in his room. That was important to him, because deep down, he wanted Brett to know someone was watching him. It was important to him that Brett know someone was interested in him. Deeply interested in him.

Brett was very close to being ready for him. Yes, indeed he was.

Time to step it up.

CHAPTER THIRTY-TWO

Fishers, Indiana

"I swear to God, somebody was in our house," Brett said in a loud whisper. "I haven't checked the basement yet, so whoever it is might still be here."

Bobby stood in the mudroom on the little rug on the inside of the door. He slipped off his shoes and stripped off his socks that were a bit damp, and he pushed his wet hair off his forehead.

He didn't exactly doubt Brett, but he could tell Brett was sincere and wasn't teasing him by the way he was acting. It just didn't make sense to him. The slider in the family room could have been opened by anyone, the same with his drawer and closet. And maybe Brett forgot about doing something with his laundry. He actually thought it was funny about Brett hiding his boxers and sock in the bottom of his basket, because he did that too when he needed to. He almost laughed out loud, but didn't dare, because Brett was so worked up.

"But how do you know for sure?" Bobby asked.

Brett rolled his eyes. "I just know. Stuff was moved, in my room. I just know, okay?"

Bobby nodded, took off his wet jacket and placed it in the dryer with the setting on low. He pushed the button for the timer for twenty minutes, and then turned around and faced his older brother.

"You checked the whole house?"

"Except for the basement. I was waiting until you came home."

Bobby swallowed and then nodded. "Okay. Let's go."

Brett led the way.

He opened up door and flipped on the light. He walked down the stairs with Bobby closely behind, their backs to the wall.

When they reached the bottom, Brett didn't turn to face him, but whispered over his shoulder and kind out of the corner of his mouth, "Wait here. I'll check around."

"I should go with you."

"No, you stay here."

Brett turned his back on him and tip-toed around, poking behind boxes, looking behind the wet bar, in the two closets, and finally in the utility room.

Nothing. No one.

Whoever was in the house, was gone.

"Hey, where are you guys?"

Both boys jumped, and then laughed.

"Uncle Tony?" Bobby said, more than a little relieved.

"What are you guys doing downstairs?"

"Nothing," Brett said, "Just looking at stuff."

Bobby turned to him and stared at him doubtfully. After all, this was a chance to tell their uncle, a cop, what had happened.

Brett took a gentle hold of Bobby's arm. "Don't say anything, okay? We don't tell anyone. This is just between you and me."

Reluctantly, Bobby nodded, and then both boys charged up the stairs.

Tony Dominico leaned against the counter with his arms folded and his gun in a holster on his belt.

"You guys want to go for pizza and some garlic bread?"

"Sure. Beats Mac n' Cheese," Bobby said.

"Just about anything beats Mac n' Cheese," Dominico said.

"Give us a second, okay?" Brett said as he led Bobby down the hallway to their bedrooms.

Brett stopped Bobby before he walked into his room. "Promise me you won't say anything, okay?"

"Don't you think we should tell someone, Mom or dad? Uncle Tony?" Bobby asked. "If someone was really here, what if he comes back?"

Brett thought for a minute, shook his head, and then said, "No. You and I just have to make sure all the doors and windows and stuff are locked up. Okay?"

"You sure, Brett?"

"Positive," Brett answered, though he didn't sound all that confident.

Bobby nodded reluctantly and then disappeared into his room to change into dry clothes.

Brett walked into his room to change. The first thing he did was to go to his dirty laundry basket and push his boxers and sock deep into his basket.

"Hiding important evidence?" Dominico said with a smile.

Brett jumped and spun around. His uncle was leaning in the doorway.

"What the hell, kid, why are you so jumpy?" he asked with a laugh. "I see that in the interrogation room and I think to myself, man, he's a guilty dude," he said with another laugh.

JOSEPH LEWIS 77

Brett felt his face getting hot, knowing he was blushing.

"No practice tonight?"

"N... no, it was raining too hard."

Dominico nodded. "You had a tough meet the other night, so it's good to take a day off."

Brett relaxed, went to the closet and pulled a clean shirt off a hanger, then slipped out of his jeans, went to his dresser, pulled open a drawer, and took out a pair of shorts and pulled them on. He sat down on the bed and took off his socks and flung them into his basket, and pushed his feet into a pair of Nike Slides.

"I'm ready."

As Brett started to walk out the door, Dominico asked, "Brett, is everything okay?"

"Yeah, sure, why?"

Dominico led him to the bed and the two of them sat down, kind of facing each other.

"Your mom told me that the death of the Grimes boy really hit you hard."

Brett looked down at his hands and shrugged.

"Why? Why does this kid's death bother you so much?" Dominico asked quietly.

Brett shrugged again. When he looked up at his uncle, he had tears in his eyes.

"It's just that he told me he didn't have anything. He said he had nothing. He said track was his way out, and now, he's dead."

Dominico put his arm around the boy and hugged him. "Brett, I deal with shit like this all the time. It never gets easy. Fathers and mothers, some of them pregnant, and sometimes, kids. It's never easy and it's never pretty."

Brett cried openly. He wiped his eyes with his hands and wiped his hands on the comforter.

"The thing is, Brett, you're still alive, and life is a gift. You can't take it for granted. And you sure as hell can't waste it."

He paused and then hugged Brett a little tighter, and kissed his forehead.

"Brett, I don't have a family of my own. You and your brother are as close to being my own two kids as I think I'll ever get. I love you guys."

He hugged him again, kissed his forehead again, and said, "You have to shake out of this funk you're in, because as long as you're in it, you're wasting time. And time shouldn't ever be wasted."

Brett made a final pass at his eyes with his hands, and then wiped his hands on the comforter.

"If this Grimes kid means this much to you, then go do something for him. Put his initials on your shoes, and when you race, you think of him, how he pushed you, and you go kick some ass in both of your names… his and yours. He can't race anymore, but you can. Go kick ass for the two of you."

Brett nodded, tried a smile on for size, but it didn't fit, so he settled for a nod, and said, "Okay. I will."

CHAPTER THIRTY-THREE

Blackduck Point, Leach Lake, Minnesota
Hide the body better, he said. *A less conspicuous location making the body less easy to find,* he said.

Fuck You!

The white paneled van drove slowly north and west over the back roads towards one of the largest inland lakes in Minnesota. The skinny man was pretty certain this area was remote enough. It certainly wasn't a conspicuous location. Hell, the only road was a dirt path, the width of a Mini Cooper, and a lot smaller than the width of the van they were in. Bushes and low-hanging branches reached out and swatted the sides of the vehicle in protest, and he was sure the paint job wouldn't survive the ride, but he didn't care. It wasn't his van.

Boosted from a parking garage in the Twin Cities for the quick trip up north, the van was a ride of convenience. Once finished with it, they'd dump the van somewhere back in the cities, probably in the long-term lot at the Minneapolis-St. Paul International Airport, where it could sit for days, even weeks, before someone noticed it.

They needed the van long enough to get rid of the kid who was handcuffed to the backseat.

Go here. Go there. Dump a kid. Pick up a kid. Dump. Pick up. Their job was pretty simple. Mindless, really. There were risks of course, but the money was good. And, there were benefits: the boys. The boys they picked up were always something they looked forward to.

"Kid, what's your name again?" The short, fat man asked.

"Fuck you!"

"Interesting name," the tall skinny man said with a laugh.

"Yeah, you talk real smart knowing you're goin' ta die today, huh smart boy?"

"Fuck you!" The boy repeated.

He was a handsome boy. Once, a strong, fast boy, from La Crosse, Wisconsin, who played football and basketball. A leader, smart, a good-natured prankster. Now, skinnier and a little taller, still blond, but his hair was a little darker. Still a handsome boy though. Smart, not that it had done him any good. No longer a prankster. It had been bled and forced out of him.

The van slowed to a stop, but the two men didn't move, nor did they utter a word. As was their ritual, they studied the area for anyone who might be nearby, for anyone who might notice them, see them.

From where they were parked, the two men could see the rocky shore and the gray-blue of the lake beyond. The water reflected the early evening of the cloudy sky. Not quite dark, not quite light. A lot of shadows.

A family of ducks and frogs singing in a weird baritone chorus of monotony that competed with the not-quite-soprano of crickets. That was it as far as life went.

"Okay, Kid. End of the line."

The boy glared at the two men. He knew what was about to happen. He had hours to prepare, hours to think about things, lots of things. Things like why, like how come him, like, well, lots of things. There weren't any answers, at least answers that made sense. Nothing had made sense. Not for the almost two years he was in captivity.

In that long trip, he decided that when the time came, he would remain quiet. He wouldn't beg. He wouldn't cry. He wouldn't give them that satisfaction.

The fat man slid open the side door, climbed in and ripped off the boy's shirt, then his shoes and socks, and then the boy's jeans and boxers. He threw all the clothes in the back of the van, along with the fast food wrappers and other assorted trash from their trip. Carefully, he removed one of the handcuffs that were attached to the backseat, and then quickly reattached it to the boy's wrist, binding both hands behind his back.

The fat man took one last look out the side door, then at the shoreline and lake beyond, to make sure no one was around, and then he grabbed the boy's arm and pulled him from the van.

The boy fell on his stomach and when he didn't get up quickly enough, the fat man kicked him. "Get up and get moving."

The boy saw the cuts to his knees and chest, but struggled to his feet, wincing at the pebbles that dug into his toes and heals. He tried to walk carefully, gingerly, but it still hurt. When he walked a short distance, still on the wooded path and not quite to the rocky shore, the fat man gave him one last shove that sent him headlong.

"On your knees," the skinny man said.

Obedient by disposition, the boy did as he was told. He shut his eyes and waited, and heard the skinny man step up behind him.

The boy didn't hear the first shot. He didn't feel the first bullet. He didn't have any thoughts. He didn't feel any pain. There was nothing but blackness, nothing but emptiness. The boy was gone and away the moment the skinny man pulled the trigger the first time.

Gone, and set free.

CHAPTER THIRTY-FOUR

Washington, D.C.
Ever since his junior year in high school, Chet didn't have any interest in sleep. He'd surf the net, write code, and had a lucrative business, designing and creating webpages. In fact, he had amassed a bank account in the mid-five figures without his parents' knowledge before he had turned seventeen, a fact he never shared with anyone. He worked quickly, quietly, and alone, because that was the most efficient way for him to work. Though he did have a loose association with any number of hackers, he stayed as far on the fringe as he could, because he didn't want to attract any negative attention.

Back then, high school and college were his day jobs. When the FBI had contacted him for an interview during his senior year at Cal Poly, they had been watching him for the better part of five years, something they didn't mention until the third interview. He had already turned them down twice, because he liked the autonomy of a solo life. But after the third interview, he was intrigued for some vague reason he couldn't put a finger on, other than perhaps gaining access to domains and corporations and internet worlds previously blocked, because of his autonomous solo life. So, he signed up.

He almost washed out of the academy because he wasn't a jock kind of guy. Far from it. But on anything academic or creative, he sat atop the class. And the top suits in the organization didn't want Chet for his physical prowess anyway. They wanted him for his mind, and especially his skill and talent in writing code, and the other things he could do with a computer.

Working for the FBI, Chet saw himself as a drone, a worker bee. He wasn't interested in moving up the food chain like Rawson or Musgrave. He saw himself as more akin to Pete, but more of a get-the-job-done-so-I-can-have-some-fun kind of guy. And his fun was done late at night, and usually alone, while the rest of the world slept.

He often worked late into the night. Ever since he found out about the kiddie porn sights, he saw it as his mission to shut them down. It didn't matter if it was one at a time, a couple of guys here, and a couple of guys there. It didn't matter if it took him away from sleep. What mattered was that these assholes and perverts were shut down. And it was in large part through his efforts that a child porn ring was shut down in New York. A police chief, a Boy Scout leader, a teacher, and a rabbi were among them. In all, more than seventy men and one woman were arrested with more to come.

Chet didn't get the credit, however, because he didn't want it. He didn't need it. He didn't care for it. He had never begun this hunt for glory. No, only the satisfaction of having put away some perverts, and in rescuing kids.

So, he passed on the fruits of his labor and all of the information he gathered to the Homeland Security Investigations arm of U.S. Immigration and Customs Enforcement anonymously. They, along with Homeland Security, set up a cyber-sting, posing as individuals interested in kiddie porn, along with sharing files and pictures. Perverts took the bait and after search warrants were issued to service providers, IP addresses were matched to hundreds of individuals. The National Center for Missing and Exploited Children were already searching the images to see if the kids in these images matched any kids from their database.

Chet felt pretty good about it, but didn't give himself a pat on the back, because he didn't have the time. There were other kids out there being exploited and used and abused, and he believed he needed to do what he could, and using whatever resources that was available to him, both the legal and the not so legal. He justified whatever he did as right and good and necessary, because he was doing it in the service of exploited kids.

So, during the day, he was a part of the small team, trying to find out who was murdering boys. At night, he worked by himself, trying to free kids from the shackles of the perverts and assholes who used them. He wasn't sure which mission was greater or the most important.

And he didn't care.

He didn't know what Pete or Summer wanted him to do and he wasn't sure where the investigation was heading, because there weren't any leads. No matter where they hunted or searched, there was nothing. What frustrated him, and what he supposed frustrated Pete and Summer, was that without admitting it to one another, without stating it out loud, they were waiting for the next boy to show up dead in the hopes that there would be a clue that would lead to someone. The problem, and the pain of it, was that in order for them to come up with a new lead, a new clue, there almost had to be another dead boy. That was the tragedy and the ethical and moral dilemma he, Pete and Summer had to wrestle with.

At just after 3:17 AM, he shut down his computer, cataloged his notes electronically in three separate places, and fell asleep in his clothes, after setting the alarm for 6:30 AM.

His day job would then begin again.

CHAPTER THIRTY-FIVE

Fishers, Indiana

"Hey, Bobby, do you mind if I sleep in here tonight?"

Brett stood at the foot of Bobby's bed, holding his pillow and a blanket, and dressed in only in boxers and shorts. Bobby was half-asleep, but awake enough to have understood Brett's question.

"Sure, I don't mind."

Brett set his pillow down on the floor at the side of the bed and crawled under his blanket. Bobby rolled over and hung over the side to see where he was.

"What are you doing down there?"

"I'm okay. Go to sleep."

Bobby stared at his brother. "You can sleep in my bed. I mean, I have a lot of room."

"You sure?"

"Yeah," Bobby said with a shrug, followed by a yawn. "I don't mind."

Brett smiled at him, got up and crawled into bed with Bobby, and lay down on his back, his eyes still open.

"What?" Brett asked, knowing Bobby was looking at him.

"Are you scared? I mean, about someone coming in the house?"

"Aren't you?"

Bobby rolled onto his side and faced his big brother.

"It's just that... I didn't think you'd be afraid of anything."

Brett shrugged. "Everybody's afraid of something."

Bobby didn't know what to say to that. It stunned him that Brett would be afraid of something, anything. He always pictured his brother as tough and invincible, afraid of nothing, willing to take on anyone or anything, and wishing that he, himself, were like that. And at the same time, Bobby didn't really know what he might be afraid of either. The only thing that came to mind was if something were to happen to his mom and dad. Death or divorce, but he didn't know why he even thought of divorce, because they seemed happy, and their family seemed happy. But there it was. It just kind of popped into his head. If his parents were to die, that might be the worst thing that could happen, though, but he was pretty sure Uncle Tony would take them in. It would still be awful, though. Really awful.

The two boys were silent for a moment or two, and then Bobby said, "Are you really sure someone was in here? I mean really, *really* sure?"

"Why else would my boxers and my sock be on top of my dirty laundry, when I know I buried them at the bottom?"

Bobby pursed his lips and thought for a minute. "Well, what if mom or dad were looking for something and dug around to look for it? That's a possibility, isn't it?"

Brett stared at Bobby. "Only my boxers and my sock were on top. Everything else was right where it should have been. I notice stuff like that."

Bobby nodded.

"Okay, so, what do we do?"

"We keep watch. We make sure the doors and windows are shut and locked before we leave for school."

"We can do that."

"And I think we should set a trap, but I don't know how, yet."

"What do you mean, a trap?" Bobby asked cautiously.

"I don't know, but I'll think of something."

Bobby nodded again.

"Don't you think we should tell mom or dad, or somebody like Uncle Tony?"

Brett shook his head. "Not yet. I want to make sure first. I mean, I'm pretty sure already, but I want to make really sure. Okay?"

Bobby nodded and then smiled.

"What?"

"I think it's funny you use a sock when you do it."

Bobby couldn't tell for sure, but he knew Brett was blushing.

"I do too," Bobby offered.

"Seriously, you use a sock, too?"

Bobby chuckled. "Yeah, I figure, who would check one of my socks. They stink."

Brett smiled. "Mine are usually sweaty, too."

They were silent for a while and then Brett said, "Thanks for helping me with my stupid poem for English."

Bobby rolled onto his back. "It's okay."

"I knew you were good at writing. You have, what... three poems published?"

"Four, but I'm working on another. I just have to come up a title."

"That's pretty cool, Bobby. How many other fourth graders can say they have something published? You could be famous someday."

Bobby turned to look at his brother to make sure Brett wasn't teasing him. When he was sure he wasn't, he smiled and said, "Thanks."

"Goodnight."

"Yeah, goodnight."

After they shifted onto their sides with their backs to each other, and with a laugh Brett said, "Hey. Don't do anything tonight that you might need a sock for, okay? That would be gross."

Bobby laughed, turned a little and said over his shoulder, "Too late," and then laughed again.

"Wait, serious?"

Bobby nodded and laughed again.

"Gross! What side of the bed were you on?"

Bobby laughed, "Kind of in the middle."

"Gross! Did you get any on the sheets?"

Bobby laughed, "Nope. I was just kidding."

Brett didn't believe him and turned over to look at him, lifted up the covers to inspect Bobby, and then rolled over. "Just don't tonight, okay?"

"I don't know. I think I'm getting a boner."

Brett laughed, and elbowed Bobby in the back. "You're gross."

And Bobby laughed some more.

CHAPTER THIRTY-SIX

Washington, D.C.
The area where Chet worked was called the bullpen. It was a large room with fifteen work stations in five rows of three across. They were penned in by boring beige moveable walls. A work station consisted of a desk, desktop computer, a couple of file cabinets and a chair on wheels. In Chet's case, he had two desktop monitors and two desktop computers, along with two laptops. He was fortunate to have a corner unit, otherwise, he would have felt claustrophobic.

Summer and Pete had offices up in the balcony that overlooked the bullpen. While he had his own desk and desktop computer, Pete shared his office with Doug Rawson, who mostly wasn't in the office. Neither Pete nor Summer knew exactly where he went or worked, thinking that Logan had him running here and there, or perhaps a suit above Logan had him running here and there.

Summer had her own office, because she was a team leader. Her office was rather small, accommodating a desk, two visitor's chairs, a window with blinds, two file cabinets and a modest bookshelf filled with law books and pictures of her mom and dad, and some college friends. Because he was a unit chief, Logan Musgrave had a larger office, two doors further down towards the corner. He had the same set up as Summer's office, but also had a small, round conference table and three chairs.

When Chet arrived at the Hoover Building that morning, Pete and Summer were already waiting for him at his cubicle. Summer sat on his chair, while Pete leaned up against the desk with his arms folded across his chest.

Pete stood up straight and smiled when he saw him. "Chet, I think we have an idea."

Summer stood up, looked out over the top of the cubicles at the rest of the bullpen, knowing that there wouldn't be a lot of privacy. She said, "Why don't you bring your laptop and we'll go to the conference room, okay?"

Chet had a leather computer bag hung over his shoulder as usual, and didn't bother to take it off. He dropped his car keys into his top drawer and followed the two of them out of the bullpen area. The three of them never said a word, choosing to walk in silence.

When they arrived at the conference room, they entered and Summer shut the door behind them. Chet noticed a map of the continental United States with colored push pins, marking the places where the four boys had been found, with one end of a piece of colored string attached to the pushpin, and the other attached to a pin under the picture of the boy who was found there.

"Someone's been busy," Chet said as he sat down and fired up his laptop. He reached into his bag and brought out another.

"Why two?" Summer asked.

"In case I have to switch between two sites. It's faster and easier for me if I do it this way."

Chet also pulled out two thumb drives and plugged one into the USB port in each of the computers.

"Okay, I'm ready."

Pete looked at Summer and then back at Chet. "Here's what I'd like you to do. For each dump site... the location where we found a body, I want you to look for any statewide Amber Alerts for boys whose ages were eleven to thirteen, either ten days previous to the body being found, to ten days after the projected time. Do this for each boy we found."

Stunned, Chet opened his mouth, eyes wide. "Jesus! That's brilliant, Pete. Why didn't we think of that sooner?" And before either Pete or Summer had an opportunity to answer, Chet's fingers flew over the keys.

"Okay, I found an alert for a boy... a Marcus Caleb Delroy, age eleven from Las Vegas, Nevada, four days after we found Brian Mullaney. Still missing, listed as suspicious circumstances."

"What race?" Pete asked.

"Caucasian," he paused at the keyboard and looked up, "Because pedophiles mostly stay within their same race, right?"

Summer nodded. "Usually, and because the other boys are Caucasian, it might mean our same perverts."

Pete went to the map and placed a different colored pushpin in the map marking the city, and then went to the whiteboard and wrote in marker the information Chet had just given them.

"Is that the only Amber Alert you found for Nevada?" Summer asked.

"Yes, at least within that time frame, and that matches our boys," Chet said, not looking up from the keyboard, fingers still flying.

He worked the laptop a while longer and said, "That's it."

Pete sighed, as did Summer.

"But wait. I found something interesting if you're looking for patterns," Chet said absentmindedly.

"What?" Summer asked.

"Okay. We found Robert Monroe in White Cloud, Michigan, but he was from Terre Haute, Indiana and that's only one state away. We found Gary Haynes in Coal Run, Ohio and he was from Michigan, again, one state away. We found Richard Clarke in Victorville, California and he was from Arizona."

"One state away," Summer finished for him.

"And we found Brian Mullaney in Nevada, and he's from California."

"All boys were found one state away from where they were taken," Summer said.

"So, it could be that they dump a kid in one state and pick up a kid in a neighboring state. Maybe," Chet said tentatively, not sure if his detective work was in the same league as Pete's or Summer's.

"Whoever is doing this..." he trailed off as he thought about it, and then said, "Possibly, they dump a body in one state and pick up a kid in a different state, like Chet said." Pete said with his back to Summer and Chet. "Or, they dump a kid in the same state where they pick a boy up," he paused, "Maybe. As nearly as we can tell."

"Maybe, as nearly as we can tell," Summer echoed.

"Guys, we might have something" He nodded and then repeated, "We might have something."

"So, when do we want to run this theory by Musgrave and Rawson?" Chet asked.

Neither Pete nor Summer answered him.

JOSEPH LEWIS 91

CHAPTER THIRTY-SEVEN

East of Round Rock, Navajo Indian Reservation, Arizona

It had been hot the night before and the new day seemed to get hotter by the minute, but that was pretty typical for the desert. And it seemed like a longer than long walk to their ranch after the bus dropped George and William off at the dirt road. As usual, George sat with Charles, but stared at Rebecca, who sat towards the front of the bus with her friends. She didn't say more than a few words to him all day. He didn't think he'd ever understand girls. But girls weren't on his mind. Somehow, beating the heat was, and he would have given just about anything to take a swim in the river that ran below the ridge, but he was certain there wasn't any water in it, because it hadn't rained for several days.

He got home, hugged and kissed his little sister Mary, and his mother and grandmother.

"Are you going to see, Nochero?" Robert asked excitedly.

"Who's Nochero?" William asked.

"George's horse," Robert answered. "A big, black stallion," he added in almost a whisper.

"He's not my horse, Robert," George said patiently. "I told you that he belongs to the desert."

"But he's your friend."

"Yes, he is my friend."

"Mine, too?" Robert asked hopefully.

George smiled. "We will see, okay?"

His mother noticed George looking around in the kitchen cupboards, and she smiled. "I already packed an apple and a carrot in your saddlebag."

"Thank you, Mother."

George's mother was pretty and short, and a little round, and like George, tended to be quiet. He wasn't sure he looked like her, but each time he looked at Mary and Robert, he saw his mother. William looked a lot like George and was nearly as tall, though skinnier, if that was possible.

George stole a piece of fry bread, and then decided to steal two pieces, and his grandmother swatted at him with a dish towel playfully.

His grandmother was even shorter and rounder than his mother, and liked to laugh and hug and kiss. When she smiled, her eyes disappeared. Her gentle and kind face was lined in a mass of bronze-colored wrinkles. Typically, and like his mother, she wore her gray hair in a long braid, tied at the end with a piece of leather. During the day, she and his mother cooked and baked, and weaved blankets, mended holes in clothes, and made jewelry out of silver, turquoise and leather, and sold them at the trading post in Teec Nos Pos.

George loved his family. His life on the small ranch with horses and sheep, in the desert surrounded by buttes and mesas was happy and healthy and loving. It was a simple life, a good life. And while they didn't have much, it didn't matter to him, because he had more than enough.

He carried his rifle, canteen and saddlebag out of the house, and stood on the top step, looking in all directions, hoping he'd see the stallion, but he didn't. He sighed, headed to the barn, and saddled up the pinto instead. He rode off along the trail meeting his grandfather halfway as usual.

"Yá'át'ééh," George said.

"Yá'át'ééh." His grandfather looked past him, and then smiled, "A very hot day."

George nodded. "Yes, very hot."

"The sheep are calm and content, as all life should be. But we know that all life is not content."

George didn't know what he meant, but waited, hoping his grandfather would further explain.

"Most *biligaana* are impatient with life. Always rushing here or rushing there," he said motioning with his hands this way and that. "They would not know peace or contentment if it bit them on the leg like a snake."

George nodded.

"The *Dine'* must not attach themselves to the *biligaana* way of rushing and hurrying. The Navajo must learn to be patient and let life come to them, and not chase after life. Life is like a hawk. It flies where it wants. It lands where it wants. There is beauty and purpose in the hawk's flight. The *Dine'* must remember that."

George sat in silence, considering his grandfather's words.

"The good *Dine'* watches and listens and notices things that most *biligaana* do not. Not all *biligaana,* but too many of them."

At last, his grandfather looked straight at George, smiled, nodded. "Yá'át'ééh."

"Yá'át'ééh," George answered.

As his grandfather rode past him, he said, "Your friend, Nochero, waits for you on the ridge."

George wanted to ask him how he knew the stallion's name, but guessed that Robert must have told him.

George rode the rest of the way in silence, considering what his grandfather said. He knew there was a purpose, a lesson, and a reason for his grandfather's words, but he didn't know what it was. At least, not yet.

He reached the stand of pines and tied the pinto to a low branch out of the sun, and because it was so hot, he took the saddle and blanket off the horse and set them in a neat pile in the shade. Then, he walked through the stand of pine to the chair made of two rocks, and set down his canteen. He reached into his saddlebag, took out the binoculars, and searched the hillside where the sheep grazed and the road that ran along it, and then swung it up towards the ridge. And there was Nochero, waiting, perhaps impatiently, for his apple and carrot.

George stepped forward, and as was his custom, whistled two sharp but melodic bursts, followed by long burst, and Nochero started down the hillside in a slow walk towards him, recognizing the whistle and his friend who had called him.

Nochero came forward and nuzzled George, who rubbed the stallion's neck and side, then produced the apple and carrot and the big horse ate first one and then the other. Then the two of them walked down among the sheep as George counted them. Not one of the sheep was missing.

George and Nochero ended back up among the stand of pines and found Rebecca, sitting on a blanket she had spread out next to the stone chair.

Ever since that night she kissed him, he had seen her in a completely different light. She was pretty, actually beautiful. He liked to look at her and he liked the sound of her voice. And as these thoughts tumbled around in his head, his stomach did a weird dance, and he felt a wonderful stirring, that same stirring he felt the night of their first kiss.

He sat down next to her. "I have an extra piece of fry bread if you want it."

She smiled. "I ate it already," she blushed, and in a quiet voice added, "And a piece of jerky."

George liked the fact she made herself at home with him.

"I was waiting for you."

He blinked and waited, trying desperately to keep any expression off his face.

She reached out, took a gentle hold of his face and kissed him on his lips. It was gentle without the urgency of the other night. She pulled back, looked up into his eyes, and kissed him again, this time, her lips parted and she used her tongue. He answered her in kind and then took her in a gentle, but hesitant embrace.

They lay down on the blanket facing each other, with Rebecca a little on top. Their kisses were long and deep, but gentle. As they kissed, Rebecca took hold of George's hand and placed it inside her shirt on her bare breast, holding it there, guiding his fingers and thumb to her nipple. Her other hand found George's bare chest and she did the same to him.

Their breathing came in shallow gasps, their kisses became more urgent and deeper, neither willing to take their lips from the other, their tongues probing gently.

While George's hand remained glued to Rebecca's breast, her hand dipped lower to his bare stomach, and then inside of his jeans, touching, caressing, and playing with his erection. Deftly, she undid the button and lowered his zipper, freeing him from the confinement of his boxers. She cupped him between his legs and he felt himself arching his back as she gently squeezed him there. Then she took gentle hold of his erection and began stroking him slowly.

George could barely breathe. He forgot he was kissing her. He forgot he was touching her breast, completely lost in what she was doing to him. If it was possible, he felt himself get harder, stiffening, almost painfully. He arched his back and at last, finished, warm and sticky on his stomach and in her hand.

Her fingers touched his lips, his tongue, and then they kissed again, mouths open, tongues probing.

He lay on his back, exposed. Her hand back down there, touching, caressing, gently squeezing, and though she still held him there, she pulled back, looked down, and smiled at him.

In not quite a whisper, she said, "You're bigger than I thought you'd be."

George blushed.

"And you have some hair."

He blushed even more.

"You're handsome."

He had wanted to tell her many things. Thoughts tumbled in his head. His heart, his head, and his body pulled him in different directions. But above and beyond it all, the words of his grandfather came back to him, *The Dine' must not attach themselves to the biligaana way of rushing and hurrying. The Navajo must learn to be patient and let life come to them and not chase after life.*

At once, he felt immense guilt at what they had done, at what he had allowed Rebecca to do. George reached down and took Rebecca's hand from him, and held it on his damp, sticky stomach. Ashamed, and not liking that feeling, he took her hand in both of his hands and tried to find the right words to say.

"What?" Rebecca asked in a whisper.

She tried to kiss him, but he pulled back. She took her hand from his and wiped it absentmindedly on her blanket.

He had a habit of speaking formally when he felt it was important to do so, and what he wanted to say; had to say, was important to him, and important for Rebecca to hear.

"Rebecca, I... I... like you a lot. More than a lot. You are my best friend," he said softly.

She drew her knees up to her chest and hugged them. Her face hardened and she stared straight ahead out over the little pasture at the sheep.

"We can't do... this. Not yet. We are too young. We need to wait. We need to be older."

George had hoped his words meant something. He didn't want to hurt her or her feelings. But she sat there, staring, not speaking. He wished she would look at him.

"Rebecca, we have known each other forever," she didn't answer, didn't move. "I like you a lot, Rebecca."

She stood up, buttoned up her shirt, and dusted her jeans off, and without looking at him, she said, "I would like my blanket."

George stood up and stepped off her blanket. He pulled up his jeans, zipped and buttoned them.

She grabbed her blanket and stormed off through the pines to her horse.

"Rebecca," George called after her, but she didn't stop. She never turned around.

CHAPTER THIRTY-EIGHT

Fishers, Indiana

He sat in his car, across the street, and two doors down from the McGovern house. The neighborhood was quiet and devoid of movement. Perhaps the rain chased everyone inside, but more than likely, it was the late hour in this bedroom community of Indy.

He was awake, though, reveling in his late-night visit, his stealth. He was a predator, and a hunter, a lethal and deadly warrior.

He waited two nights for this little foray and had just returned to his car from his little visit inside the McGovern home. He loved the challenge, the thrill, and the excitement of it. Mostly, he loved watching Brett and Bobby sleep. He loved that a lot.

Bobby slept curled on his left side, covers kicked off, in his boxers and shorts, his back and stomach bare.

He stood over him, listening to Bobby breathe, with his mouth slightly open, and a half-smile on his face, as if he had known a secret he wasn't about to tell anyone. His chestnut brown hair mussed, his face angelic, cute, and beautiful.

Bobby was a heavy sleeper, so he was able to touch Bobby's face, gently. Then he went to his dirty laundry basket and searched for what he thought might be there. He took it, and felt it, a little crusty, but still a little moist. He laid it on top of all the dirty laundry, so Bobby would find it.

He then went to Brett's room, saving his room for last, saving that image, that picture, that memory to be replayed over and over, and perhaps, embellished upon.

A heavy sleeper like his brother, he knew Brett was tough to wake up, even after a good night's sleep.

Brett had been on his back, a bit spread-eagled, a sheet covering his knees and feet. His hair, the same color and cut of his younger brother, slightly mussed, as Bobby's had been. His eyes, shut with a slight grimace on his adorable, handsome face.

He wanted so much to kiss his lips and to do so much more.

Instead, he stood over him, staring at Brett's pecs, his stomach, well-muscled, for a fifth grader.

A noticeable bulge under his shorts, lifting them as a pole would lift a tent.

He couldn't help himself, so he reached out and touched it. He gripped it lightly, and stroked it. He had noticed Brett's breathing change, his stomach tighten, a twitch of his right hand, his dominant hand.

He had wanted to continue until just the right moment when nature would take over, but he knew Brett might wake up, and then the little game would be lost. Someday, however, someday.

The thought thrilled and excited him.

His last stop had been to Brett's laundry basket. He searched it until he found what he was looking for, and then he placed both items on top, where Brett would notice them. In the morning, both Brett and Bobby would compare notes, and they would know that someone had been there while they slept, someone who watched them, leaving them to wonder what else that someone might have done. Or perhaps, might do, when the time was right.

He sat in his car, fighting the urge to go back into the house and do it again, but he knew that would be pushing his luck. No, he'd come back another night, for yet another visit, one that would produce wonderful and delightful results. Maybe a night when he, and they, would do so much more.

And that thought excited him.

He drove off leaving the quiet neighborhood and its inhabitants the peaceful slumber he didn't want them to have.

CHAPTER THIRTY-NINE

Blackduck Point, Leach Lake, Minnesota

Steve Bolling couldn't get that curiosity out of his head. That other day, that twilight time between day and night, he had given into his favorite pleasure and had tucked his Crestliner Sportfish into a small inlet, in search of walleye, when he saw the headlights on the shore. His first thought that it was a couple of teenagers looking for the middle of nowhere in order to play a little grab ass, something he had done at that age many moons ago. What had thrown him off and made him more than a little curious were what sounded like firecrackers. He thought they might have celebrated their little poke and tickle by giving themselves their own little fireworks show.

Perhaps, perhaps not. It didn't quite make sense to him. It didn't seem right, but he also knew teenagers were a bit weird nowadays, a lot weirder than any kids he knew or hung around with back in the day.

He let those thoughts percolate until he felt compelled to satisfy that curiosity. So, he changed into his swimsuit, an old t-shirt, and his Teva water shoes. He told his wife, Margaret, that he'd be back for supper, and let the screen door slam shut as he crossed the backyard, walked down his newly installed aluminum pier, climbed into his mistress, fired up the 125 horsepower Evinrude, and sped off for Blackduck Point.

It took him just over twenty minutes from his slip to the little snub-nosed rocky peninsula. He had been watching his depth finder and noticed he was coming up on rocks, so he cut the engine, coasted in a little further, and then dropped the anchor twenty-five yards out. He jumped in and dog-paddled the rest of the way to shore.

He was in reasonably good shape for a fifty-seven-year-old, so the distance didn't tax him, and when he could stand and carefully walk in among the rocks, he wasn't even huffing and puffing.

He wiped what remained of the warm lake water out of his eyes, checked himself over for leaches, didn't find any, and started up the shore. He climbed over rocks, big and small, to the dirt and gravel road where he believed the teenagers had been.

He was so intent on his footing he didn't see the boy's body until he was less than ten yards away.

He gasped and gagged, and then gave up, leaned over a rock, and threw up. When he finished, he straightened himself up, wiped his mouth with the back of his hand, and backed up and sat down on a rock. He couldn't take his eyes off the little boy bent over like he was meditating. Only he wasn't meditating. He was dead.

CHAPTER FORTY

Blackduck Point, Leach Lake, Minnesota

Pete and Summer felt sick, tired and frustrated, but mostly angry. After they received the phone call, they jumped on a jet out of Reagan National and flew into Minneapolis-St. Paul. From there, they took a helicopter to Black Duck, where the State Patrol met them and drove them with sirens screaming and blue lights flashing to the death scene.

There were no whip marks or brand, but everything about the boy was the same. He had been found nude with his hands cuffed behind his back, and with two shots to the back of his head. There was no doubt in Pete's or Summer's mind that an autopsy would show prolonged sexual abuse as well.

Both turned and looked at the older man in the swim trunks sitting on a rock with a towel wrapped around his shoulders, head down, as if somehow the rocky shore held the answers to any number of questions that played over and over in his head.

Summer turned to the most senior of the state patrolmen and asked, "Did you interview him?"

"Yes. We also recorded it and we have his written statement for us as well."

On a hunch, Pete pulled out his cell and punched in Chet's number. "Chet, can you check for any Amber Alerts for Minnesota in the last forty-eight hours?" Pete said.

"I'll get right on it," he paused and then said, "Was the boy found like the others?"

Pete muttered. "Exactly like the others. Crime techs aren't here yet, but I'm sure all the circumstances will be the same as the other boys."

"Shit, Pete. What the hell?"

"I know."

He clicked off and then to the two state patrol officers standing nearby, said, "I'd like to get photographs of the crime scene, especially the tire marks here and there," he said pointing to the ground near his feet.

"Our crime techs are on the way and should be here in less than twenty minutes," the older of the two said.

Pete and Summer slipped on white plastic booties and green surgical gloves, and carefully, so as not to contaminate any evidence, stepped over to the boy's body to take a closer look.

"Do you have a clear look at his face?" Pete asked Summer, "I don't."

"No, neither do I."

Pete's cell buzzed, so he reached into his pocket and saw who it was. "What have you got, Chet?"

"Pete!" Chet yelled. "An Amber Alert went out two hours ago. Casey Wayne Babbitt, age eleven is missing from Rochester, Minnesota."

"How long has he been missing?"

"I checked that, too. The reports say he's been missing seven hours. He was coming home from baseball practice. Someone found his bike, his baseball glove, and his cleats on the sidewalk. They knew it was Casey Babbitt because his name was written in permanent ink on his glove, and his initials were on the tongue of his cleats. Why it wasn't called in sooner, God only knows! I mean, what the hell? That isn't suspicious enough?"

"Chet, good work, but I gotta go. Keep me posted on any developments."

Chet started to say something, but Pete cut the phone call off before he knew what it was.

He turned to the state patrolmen. "Where is Rochester from here?"

The older of the two answered, "Maybe three or so hours from here, south and east."

"What's happened, Pete?"

"Summer, a boy was taken in Rochester, Minnesota twelve hours ago. An Amber Alert went out two hours ago."

Summer shut her eyes and shook her head in frustration. "Twelve hours ago? He could be anywhere by now."

"Call Quantico, see if we can get the Rapid Response Team on this."

"Pete, I don't know—"

"I'm calling in a favor. Just do it."

Pete turned his back, walked a short distance away out of earshot from anyone who might overhear him, and punched a number into his cell. It was picked up after two rings.

"Pete, what's up?"

"Whitey, I need a favor."

"What's happened?"

Pete brought him up to speed with all they had, knowing he would have been briefed in weekly reports with at least the basics already. Pete told him about the boy they just found, about the Amber Alert, and finished with his theory, leaving Summer's and Chet's names out of it. If there was going to be any blowback, he wanted it on him, not them.

"I'd like to get Rapid Response in here ASAP."

"I'll make the call now. And Pete, good work so far, even if it is being discounted down below."

"Politics."

"Yes, unfortunately. A fact of life in this organization. No worries on my part. You just keep doing what you do. I have your back."

"I know." Pete paused, "Whitey?"

"Yeah?"

"Thanks. I appreciate it."

He clicked off and walked over to Summer and her expression was one of anger and frustration, but she controlled her words.

"They said the local authorities hadn't invited them yet."

"That's about to change," Pete said quietly. "Give them five minutes and then call them again with the same request."

Summer looked at him doubtfully, wanted to ask him a question or two, but decided not to. So instead, she redialed Quantico.

"Yes," she turned to Pete in surprise. "Yes. That's good. We'll meet you there," she clicked off the cell, turned to Pete and said, "Let's go!"

CHAPTER FORTY-ONE

East of Round Rock, Navajo Indian Reservation, Arizona

While he was normally quiet, he was even more so today. George spent most of the day alone, stuck in his own thoughts as he tried to sort out his feelings.

On the bus ride to school, his normal bus seat partner, Rebecca's brother, Charles, sat with a couple of other sixth graders, so George sat by himself. He wanted to talk to Rebecca, to apologize, but she didn't even look in his direction. Once at school, she'd dart out of and into classrooms, and after his third hour class, he gave up trying. At lunch, he sat with the guys, but didn't participate in their conversations or laugh at their jokes. She sat two tables away and never made eye contact, at least that he could tell.

He finished up his lunch and took his tray to the window where the cafeteria service ladies would collect them, and wash them, and as he was leaving, his counselor Elizabeth Two Deer, approached him.

"George, can I speak with you a moment?"

George's stomach dropped, his mouth dried up like it was filled with cotton balls, and he couldn't swallow. He had the sudden urge to throw up the hotdog, baked beans, and fruit cup he had just eaten. Unable to speak, he nodded. He was petrified Rebecca told her about what they had done.

"Mr. Danforth, Ms. Crandall and I have an idea we think you might be interested in."

George relaxed a little, but not much. Danforth was his English teacher and favorite teacher, and Crandall was his science teacher, who everyone liked. He didn't know what sort of idea they had or if it was just a way to get him to her office where they'd gang up on him.

"Could you come with me to my office? They're waiting for us."

George looked over at Rebecca who stared at the two of them as they spoke in the corner of the cafeteria. When he saw her, she quickly turned back to her friends, but glanced at him once or twice before he followed Ms. Two Deer to her office.

When they reached her office, he could hear Danforth and Crandall laughing about something. Two Deer ushered him in and sat behind her desk. Danforth stood to greet him, and showed him to a chair set by itself in front of the other two. The office was so cramped, their knees almost touched his.

"Am I in trouble?" George asked quietly.

"Of course!" Danforth said. "You're such a desperado!" He and Crandall laughed and Crandall gave George's shoulder a gentle, good-natured shove.

In addition to the books the language arts class had to read like *Hoot*, *Wonder*, and *Gooseberry Park*, Robin Danforth gave George credit for and would discuss Tony Hillerman novels, featuring Leaphorn and Chee, two Navajo policemen. These discussions interested George, because it gave him an opportunity to talk about Navajo history and culture, and he appreciated the fact that Danforth asked him questions and seemed genuinely interested in the *Dine'*. But even with his joke, George wasn't totally relaxed.

"I've been going over your end of year testing, and you've done very, very well, George," Two Deer said pleasantly. "And, I've been looking at your career interest survey. It seems you have a high interest in criminal justice and psychology."

Two Deer was of the Ute nation, sort of a second cousin to the Navajo. She was dark, short and round, and like George, had long black hair. But she wore her hair in a long ponytail, where as George let his long hair hang neatly on his shoulders and down his back. George would smile every time she smiled, because her eyes disappeared behind her long eyelashes.

He had no idea what psychology was and he must have looked confused, because Crandall said, "Psychology is the study of human behavior. Psychology seeks to find the answer to why humans do what they do."

George nodded. Yes, he was interested in that. He and his grandfather would have long discussions about human nature and behavior.

"The three of us have been talking, George, because we see some real potential in you that we don't usually see in many students," Two Deer said.

"You do really well in science and your test scores show that," Crandall said. "You ask insightful, deep questions that I don't even get from many of the high school students."

"I've noticed the same thing in language arts," Danforth said. "You have a knack for writing, and for being able to analyze different points of view. I noticed that when there is a class discussion, you usually do more listening than talking, but I know you're listening because when you do say something, you come up with some powerful points and arguments."

"You and I've talked about what you might do after high school, and you mentioned that you might want to go to college," Two Deer said.

George was noncommittal. He knew his cousin Leonard only had an associate degree from a community college and was a Navajo Nation Policeman. George also knew that his family couldn't afford much of anything by way of college. More than likely nothing at all.

Like a good Navajo, he kept any expression from his face, but something must have shown through, or perhaps Danforth guessed at what he was thinking.

"George, there are many scholarships and grants out there for minority youth, especially for students with excellent grades."

"And you're a fine student, George. One of the best I've ever had," Crandall said.

Forest Crandall was old and stooped, but friendly. He had wild white hair that seemed to stick out no matter if he combed it or not. George liked him, because he was kind and because he cared about the students. When there was a basketball game or baseball game, Crandall and his wife would be there, yelling and cheering and congratulating the athletes whether or not they won.

He always began class with a joke. Students would groan and complain, but they would ask at the start of each class what his joke of the day was.

"So, here's what we'd like to do," Two Deer said. "Mr. Danforth is going to give you books that will push you and pull you a little, about things you're interested in."

"I thought we'd start with a little Sherlock Holmes," Danforth said handing him a heavy, thick red book with two characters on the cover. "Holmes is one of my favorite characters. He and his partner, Doctor Watson, solve crimes that Scotland Yard can't solve."

"Scotland Yard is a famous law enforcement agency in England, sort of like our FBI," Crandall explained.

"Sir Arthur Conan Doyle started out writing for magazines, and then they became serialized. This means the stories are short. I think you might have a little difficulty because the English is England English, and old English at that, but you and I can talk after each story."

George flipped through the book, stopping on a page with a drawing, and then moving on to another page with a drawing. Then he smiled at his English teacher and nodded.

"I have an even better idea for science," Crandall said with a smile, his eyes twinkling. He reached down into a bag and pulled out a small electronic device.

"This is a Samsung Touch Screen Notepad, a little better than the one we use here at school."

George set the Holmes book on the floor by his feet, and held the small computer gently.

Crandall held out a small thumb drive and George took it.

"You and I are going to spend a little time together, so I can show you how to use this, so don't worry. All I ask is that you take care of this while you use it. First thing each morning, bring it to me and I'll recharge it for you. At the end of the day, before you get on the bus, stop by and take it."

George nodded.

"Now, on this thumb drive, I've loaded several episodes of two television shows I think you're going to enjoy. At least, my wife and I enjoy them. One is called, *Criminal Minds*, which is about a group of FBI profilers, who go out and try to solve mysterious crimes. They study human behavior. The other show is called, *CSI*, and it stands for Crime Scene Investigation. That's something Robin... I mean, Mister Danforth tells me you like about Chee and Leaphorn."

George smiled and nodded, glancing at Danforth.

"After lunch, you, Mister Danforth, and I can discuss the episodes. If you want, you can even bring your lunch to my classroom and we can talk while we eat."

"We can do the same after you read one of the stories in the Holmes anthology. Maybe alternate days."

"We only have a couple of weeks left of school before summer, but this can give us a nice start to your sixth grade."

"So, what do you think?" Two Deer asked.

George didn't know what to say. All he could do was smile, in part because of what his teachers gave him, and in part because he wasn't in trouble.

Danforth, Crandall, and Two Deer settled for his nod and smile.

Before he left, Danforth placed a hand on George's shoulder, gave it a gentle squeeze and said, "You're a smart young man. More importantly, you're a good young man. I'm looking forward to this."

"Thank you, Sir."

Crandall elbowed Danforth and said, "You have to admit that my gift is better than his, right?"

JOSEPH LEWIS 107

George blushed. He wasn't about to choose one over the other, because he liked both gifts and both men.

Crandall gave him a wink and followed Danforth out the door.

The rest of the day, George had forgotten about Rebecca. He couldn't wait to begin reading the Holmes book, and he couldn't wait to see what was on the electronic notebook.

He retrieved both from is locker, stuffed them into his backpack, and headed down the hall and the front door of the school where the buses waited.

He felt a firm grip and a tug on his arm, and he turned and stood face to face with Rebecca.

"What did they want?"

George blinked, surprised that she was speaking to him after a full day of trying to avoid him.

"Well?"

He shook his head, "Nothing. Mr. Danforth gave me a book and Mr. Crandall gave me an electronic notebook."

She squinted at him trying to decide if he was telling the truth, and George knew it.

He set his jaw, glared at her. "I do not lie."

At that, she turned, stormed off, went out the door to the bus.

George stared after her, annoyed that she thought he might be lying to her. He followed her, boarded the bus and didn't even look at her the entire trip home.

CHAPTER FORTY-TWO

Fishers, Indiana

After waking up and finding what had been placed on top of their dirty laundry, the boys panicked. Brett walked into Bobby's room holding his boxers and sock, and Bobby answered by holding up his own sock from his dirty laundry.

Brett whispered, "Don't say anything to mom or dad. I want to think about his, okay?"

Bobby's first instinct was to tell both of his parents, but he reluctantly agreed not to.

After they got home from school, Brett and Bobby huddled in Bobby's room. At first neither said anything, but stared at one another, and then Brett began to pace.

"I think it's a guy, don't you?"

Bobby nodded. He couldn't picture a woman breaking in. In his mind, that was a guy thing.

"Okay. Then, how did he know you... you know... *did* it?"

Bobby turned deep crimson and shrugged. He was embarrassed that somebody had caught him.

"The only way I can think of was that someone was watching you through the window."

Horrified, Bobby said, "Oh my God! That's so gross!" Then he thought a bit and said, "Well, how did he know you did it? Maybe he was watching you, too."

"But I actually *didn't do* anything. I had a wet dream. I wiped it off with my sock and then I changed boxers."

"Oh. I didn't know."

Brett shrugged. "So, I guess, he must have been watching me too. How else would he know, right?"

Bobby nodded thoughtfully, and then said, "So, who do you think it is?"

"No idea."

Brett stood near Bobby's desk with his hands on his hips, his lips pursed.

"I think we should tell someone, Brett. This is pretty creepy. I think mom and dad need to know."

Brett looked at him and considered the suggestion. *Perhaps Bobby was right, but what could they actually say? Other than socks and boxers, what proof did they have? And, did either of them really want to talk about that stuff to their mom and dad?* That was private stuff. Nobody ever talked about that stuff with anyone, especially a mom and dad. Maybe a brother, possibly a best friend, maybe. But mostly nobody, because it was private.

"Not mom and dad, maybe Uncle Tony. He's a cop, so he'd know what to do."

Both boys were smart, perhaps Bobby more so. He knew why Brett hesitated to tell their mom and dad, and he knew it was a catch twenty-two. First of all, the doors and windows had been locked. They made sure of it before they went to bed. *So, the question was, how did he get in?* Secondly, neither of them wanted to wave socks and boxers around, especially to their mom and dad, advertising what they do sometimes in the dark of the night when they are alone.

Brett was right. They were stuck and they knew it. The only person they could tell who might understand would be Uncle Tony.

Bobby nodded. "So, when do we tell him?"

Brett pulled on his lower lip and frowned. Finally, he said, "Tomorrow, I'll call him. Tonight, I'm going to the Pacers playoff game with Coach Coleman and Austin. If we say something tonight, he'll freak out and I might not get to go to the game," then he paused and said, "That okay?"

"Sure, but I think we should tell him together, don't you? If we both tell him, he might believe it. If just one of us tells him, he might think one of us is nuts."

"Okay. That's the plan then. What are you doing tonight?"

"Zach and Brandon and I are going to a movie, and we're spending the night at Zach's house."

"Okay, that's good. We'll be out of the house. If just mom and dad are here, whoever it is probably won't come."

At least he hoped that would be the case.

CHAPTER FORTY-THREE

Rochester, Minnesota

Summer and Pete met with Earl and Bertie Babbitt, parents of Casey, who were understandably distraught and frantic. Earl paced the kitchen nonstop, flinging his arms, running his hands through his thinning sandy-blond hair. He was short and slim, young looking, and the picture of Casey they had given Pete showed a mirror image of the father.

Bertie, an older sounding name for a young-looking mother, blond like her son, with blue eyes like her son, with a smile like her son, though she wasn't smiling now. Instead, her face looked hollow, gaunt, and empty. She alternated between crying and worrying, wondering who might have taken her son.

Rapid Response was on sight. They had fanned out and with the help of the Rochester Municipal Police Department, canvassed the neighborhood in a five-mile radius collecting statements, focusing on Casey's friends and their parents. So far, nothing, other than he had been at practice and while other guys had walked, rode bikes, or were driven to the park, none of them had seen Casey since the practice had ended.

One teammate, Jacob Enders, was parked at the stoplight where he saw Casey's bike, glove and cleats in a spill on the sidewalk. Just as the light turned green, Jacob jumped out of the car much to the horror of his mother who had picked him up after practice, and much to the ire of the drivers stuck behind her car that wasn't moving on the green.

That was the only lead they had, and it wasn't any lead at all.

No one could think of anyone who might have taken the eleven-year-old boy. The likely candidates sat for interviews with FBI profilers, allowed their homes to be searched, and their electronics browsed.

Nothing.

The fact that Casey had been missing for more than sixteen hours didn't help. And factor in that I-90 ran east and west out of Rochester, to join up with I-94 in Wisconsin and I-35 to the west that ran to either the Twin Cities in the north or Iowa to the south, the boy could be anywhere by now. And that didn't take into account all the possible back roads, farms, or forests, basements, cellars, or closets.

That is, if he were still alive.

Rapid Response operated under their guidelines they worked to find the boy until Hostage Rescue was called in when the boy was found.

But it was Pete's and Summer's belief that Casey wouldn't be found and was gone to whatever hell the rest of the boys were in, with the only relief, sadly, being death.

CHAPTER FORTY-FOUR

East of Round Rock, Navajo Indian Reservation, Arizona
Like he did for any reading assignment, George pulled out his notebook and a pen, and dove into the heavy red volume, beginning with *The Red-Headed League*, which was the first story Danforth wanted him to read. He sat on a hard-backed chair at one end of the kitchen table with a kerosene lantern, which gave him a fair amount of light. His mother sat at the other end mending a hole in the knee of one of William's jeans. She'd hum to herself as she sewed, but George didn't recognize any of the tunes.

"Is that a good book?" she asked in between hums.

George looked up and smiled at her. "It's a mystery."

"Ah, I see," she said with a smile and a nod.

"This is a book with a lot of stories about two detectives. One is really smart, tall and skinny. The other is a doctor, and kind of old, short and fat. He does not seem very smart, but he is funny. I think the tall man is smarter."

"I see," she said again.

"Their names are Sherlock Holmes and Doctor Watson."

"Interesting names, these two detectives."

George read a little, made some notes in his notebook, and read some more. He looked up, frowning at the window.

"I see this book has you puzzled," his grandfather was sitting in the stuffed chair by the fire, smoking his pipe.

"Yes, Grandfather. It makes me think."

"Thinking is good exercise."

George went back to his book, made some more notes, stifled a yawn, and then stretched.

"Exercise makes one tired, even if it is the exercise of one's mind," his grandfather said through a puff of his pipe.

George smiled at him. "I will go check on the sheep and the horses, and then go to bed."

"Perhaps your friend is outside waiting for you."

"I don't know. He comes and goes."

"Lately, your friend has been more coming than going," his grandfather said with a smile.

George laughed, "Maybe."

"Perhaps your friend would like a late-night snack of oats. A handful would not hurt your friendship. Food is always good for a friend."

Not bothering with a shirt, George pulled on his boots and his hat, and slipped out the door, careful not to let the screen door slam, because he didn't want to wake up Rebecca, Robert, or his grandmother who were all dozing on the couch. William was nowhere to be seen, so George assumed he was out near the barn with the horses.

George walked quietly to the pen that held the sheep, opened the door, and walked in after closing the pen behind him. He spoke softly and walked slowly, because he didn't want to alarm them. Instead, they'd nuzzle him and brush up against his leg as he moved through them.

After determining that all was safe, he left the pen and searched in both directions for Nochero, and not seeing him, whistled for him to see if he'd come.

And he did it at a slow walk, as if he was just waiting for an invitation.

They walked towards each other, and this time, Nochero didn't stop, but came right up to George.

"He's beautiful." William had appeared out of the darkness near the barn.

"He's still wild, but I think he trusts me."

"Do you think I could come closer?"

George remembered how Nochero reacted with Robert, so he said, "I think so. Just move slowly. No sudden moves."

And William did what George suggested and stood next to George, staring at the big stallion.

Nochero's nostrils flared. He stamped his front leg, but nodded.

"I think he wants you to come closer," George said softly.

William advanced tentatively, and evidently didn't move fast enough, because Nochero stepped up to him, sniffing his bare stomach.

William laughed, reached out a hand, and scratched the horse's neck, petting it, smoothing its mane, then moving to the stallion's back and flank.

"A strong horse."

George nodded. "Grandfather said I should feed him a handful of oats."

"Do you think he'll follow you?"

"Well, let's see."

William stepped back, and George turned his back on the horse, and called to it softly, using his whistle, though this time, much softer and quieter.

And Nochero followed him all the way to the barn, stopping only long enough for George to open the door. The other horses called to each other, perhaps to the stallion, as it entered as if it were his home.

George turned to William, laughed and said, "Well, look at that!"

George went to the side of the barn, where an empty stall was, found the oat bucket and brought out two hands full. Nochero chomped them down and nuzzled George's stomach with his nose.

"Good boy," George said softly. "Good boy."

"Have you ridden him yet?"

George shook his head. "Not yet."

William was nearly identical to George, though a year and a little younger, just a little shorter, and if possible, thinner. He sat down on a bale of hay, pulled one loose, stuck it into his mouth, and stretched his legs out in front of him.

George sprawled next to him, watching the three horses get to know one another.

"Do you ever think about leaving here? Going away?" William asked.

George considered the question and recognized that Rebecca had asked sort of the same question a day or so before. And having thought about it since, he had come to the same conclusion.

"No, not really."

"I'm going to leave after high school. I think I'll join the Marines or the Army."

"Really?"

William sat up straight, took the piece of straw out of his mouth, held it in his hand and said, "There's nothing to do here. We go to school. We watch sheep. We eat. Go to bed. And then, watch more sheep."

"It's a good life."

"It's a boring life. If I join the Marines, I can go places and do things, and no more sheep."

"But we wouldn't see you."

William got himself more comfortable as lightning flashed through the open barn door, followed by a low roll of thunder.

"I'd visit. And you can visit me."

George thought for a minute as another bolt flashed, followed quickly by thunder. Rain hit hard on the barn roof, and as he looked out the barn door. He could barely see the house or sheep pen, because the sky had opened up as it sometimes does in the desert in springtime.

"Do you really think you could kill someone?"

William shrugged nonchalantly, though George knew from his expression that he took the question seriously.

"If someone shot at me."

"What if your captain told you to open fire, even if no one was shooting at you?"

"Well, if they were the enemy, yes. And I'd have to follow orders."

George was pretty sure how he felt. It was wrong to kill anyone under any circumstances, but he said nothing.

"Taking one's life is a serious thing," Grandfather stood in the doorway, holding two towels and a bar of soap. "Taking one's life is serious, an order from someone or no order from someone."

"But Grandfather, if I am at war, and if I am defending my country and protecting myself, isn't it okay if I shoot at someone?"

Their grandfather nodded thoughtfully, was silent for a bit as he stared at Nochero. Then he looked back at his two grandsons. "I did not say it was okay or not okay. I did not say it was wrong or right. I said taking one's life is a serious thing."

Neither boy said anything, but George noticed William was not happy.

"I see your friend has made himself at home," Grandfather said with a chuckle.

"We fed him oats."

Grandfather nodded thoughtfully. "Your mother would like you to bathe in Mother Earth's rain. She said that you should place your dirty clothes on the porch. She put clean clothes for you there. She placed a pan of water on the porch for you to wash your feet."

He turned and stood in the doorway, and then walked into the rain in the direction of the house.

William spit out the straw in his mouth, shook his head, and went to the doorway of the barn. He stripped out of his boots, socks, jeans and boxers. Then he bundled them up, grabbed one of the towels and the soap, and sprinted towards the house.

George watched him disappear behind a curtain of driving rain. Somehow, he felt as if William was angry with their grandfather, but he didn't know why.

Nochero nudged his back with his nose and then stood tall next to him, facing the barn door.

"If you would like to stay here and keep warm and dry, you can. But you are free to go if you choose."

Nochero stomped a foot, snorted, nodded and then walked out of the barn and into the rain.

Like William, George stripped out of his clothes, bundled them and the remaining towel with one hand, shut the barn door with the other, and ran towards the porch.

He placed his clothes next to William's, and then joined his brother, who was soaping up a discreet distance from the house, and away from the windows.

"If you go into the Marines and leave, I will miss you, William."

William stopped soaping up, looked at George and said, "I don't think you will. I don't think anyone else will either."

He then turned his back on George, walked off a short distance, and began to wash his hair. When he was done, he handed George the soap.

George took hold of William's arm and held it. He saw that William was crying and that hurt George.

"William, you're wrong. I will miss you very much."

William shook out of George's grasp and said, "I doubt it," and then walked away.

George stood in the rain with his face tilted up towards the sky as another lightning flash lit up the darkness. Thunder rolled towards him and instead of flinching, and running for shelter, he stood in the rain and wept.

CHAPTER FORTY-FIVE

East of Round Rock, Navajo Indian Reservation, Arizona

Nochero screamed in the night. Sheep hollered. William was already sitting up in bed, rubbing his eyes, with Robert pressed against him.

"What's happening?" George asked in a whisper as he raised himself to a sitting position.

William shook his head and Robert stared at him, eyes wide and his mouth in a perfect O.

George jumped out of bed, pushed his feet into his moccasins, ran out of the bedroom and grabbed the rifle that stood by the kitchen door. He ran out onto the porch, letting the screen door slam behind him.

The pen gate was open and sheep were wandering all over the yard. Nochero reared and screamed, and as George stared in amazement, he caught a glimpse of the taillights of a pickup disappear down the driveway.

"William, I need your help!" he shouted over his shoulder.

He heard whispers and words coming from deeper in the house.

"William, help me!" he yelled again.

William came crashing out of the house and stood next to George.

"Round up the sheep. Someone was here, and I think they stole some. I'm going after them."

Without waiting for a response and without any further thought, George jumped on Nochero's back from behind. He yelled, "Haw!" and they took off.

It wasn't until he was halfway down the road that he realized he was riding bareback on a half-wild horse he barely knew. He crouched low and hung on to the big stallion's neck with one arm, gripping the Winchester .22 with the other, dressed only in boxers and moccasins.

Fortunately, George had been riding horses with and without a saddle from the time he could walk, and he rode well. He clung to the stallion's neck and pinched his knees and legs like any skilled rider would.

From the moment George had jumped on his back, and even before George yelled, "Haw!" Nochero had taken off like a rocket, faster and more powerful than any horse he had ever ridden. And somehow, Nochero knew where he was going.

Keeping the glow of the pickup's taillights in sight, George and Nochero followed at a distance that was growing no matter how fast and hard Nochero galloped. Nochero cut to the right and George knew that cut would take him parallel to the dirt track that the pickup would eventually turn on. He also knew there was a ravine that he and Nochero were coming up on. Because of the speed at which they traveled, the dark and the rain, he had no idea where it was.

And all at once, the big horse was airborne with George on top. It was both frightening and exhilarating, but George didn't panic. He hung on and trusted the big horse. Nochero made the landing soft and bolted up ahead trying to make up ground.

George could see the pickup clearly now. He recognized the passenger as the young Mexican, who tried to steal sheep earlier that week. He noticed George chasing him and in response to seeing George, he raised a rifle out of the window.

One shot, a second. Both wide and high.

Nochero dodged to the right, then back to the left closing the distance between them. George knew a curve in the road was coming up quickly and he had to act fast, because once that truck hit gravel, he'd lose them.

Timing it just right and holding onto the horse with just his knees and legs, George put the rifle to his bare shoulder and pulled the trigger once, and then twice. His second shot found its mark in the right front tire. The driver, the older Mexican, lost control and at the speed with which the pickup was moving, there was no way they could make the turn.

And they didn't.

It flew off the dirt road, up and over the ditch, landed and rolled once, then twice, and settled on its roof sending dirt and mud everywhere.

George watched as one of the sheep in the truck bed leapt to safety, while the other, what looked like a year-old lamb, tumbled out.

Nochero came to an easy stop and George jumped off and ran to the pickup, pointing the gun at the two men. Because of the dark, he couldn't tell for sure if they were dead or alive. Neither of them moved, and one was toppled on top of the other in a jumbled mess.

As George stood up, he noticed a pair of headlights coming his way.

He stepped to the middle of the dirt road and flagged them down, suspecting it was his grandfather and William.

William jumped out of the truck before it came to a stop, ran up to George and asked, "Are you okay?"

George nodded, but looked past him at his grandfather as he got out of the truck.

Loud enough so both, mostly his grandfather, could hear, he said, "They shot at me. I shot back and hit their tire. They lost control. I don't know if they're dead."

His grandfather walked to the upside-down truck, got down on one knee and spoke to them in Spanish.

George heard moans and cursing. Two different voices, so he knew they were alive.

And that was the first time he noticed the lamb crying.

George handed the rifle to William. "Help Grandfather, but be careful. One of them had a rifle," and then he ran to the young lamb that lay in the dirt crying.

George bent down to tend to it, and spoke soothingly to it. One leg was bent in a way it shouldn't have been and George knew it was broken. What he didn't know was how bad it was or if it could be fixed.

He sighed. All he wanted to do was get the sheep back. He didn't mean for the men to get hurt, and he didn't mean for the lamb to suffer.

It wasn't a very Navajo thing to do, but for the second time that night, he wept.

William had the two men under the aim of the rifle. Grandfather had taken the other rifle and brought it back to George.

The two of them stared at one another, and it was George who looked away first, wiping his eyes as he did so.

"Are you alright, my Grandson?"

"Yes, Grandfather."

His grandfather stared at George a little longer, looking him up and down, and then took a gentle hold of George's chin. "Can you get the sheep back to the ranch?"

"Yes, Grandfather."

Grandfather nodded. "Keep watch on these two while William and I load them into the truck. I will take them to the hospital in Chinle. I think they have broken bones."

George wanted to say something, apologize for what he had done, try to further explain what happened. But after his grandfather handed him the

Mexican's rifle, he turned his back on him. With William's help, he pulled the two men from the truck and helped them get into the bed of his grandfather's truck.

George stood there, not even bothering to point the rifle at them. Neither could move fast or far enough to get away.

He turned his back on them, and still holding the rifle, he picked up the lamb as gently as he could and set it up on his shoulders as the lamb cried, and then he started the long walk back to the ranch with the other sheep following.

Then Nochero did something odd.

He blocked George's path. When George tried to move around him, Nochero blocked that route too.

"What? What are you doing?" George shouted.

Nochero turned his side to George and nodded. Again, George tried to move around him, but Nochero backed up and blocked him.

Then it dawned on him and he set the lamb on Nochero's back and with one hand on the lamb to steady it, and with the other on the rifle, they set off on foot towards the ranch with the other sheep following obediently.

CHAPTER FORTY-SIX

East of Round Rock, Navajo Indian Reservation, Arizona

The heavy rain gave way to a light mist, and George's mother was waiting on the porch to stay out of it, but when she saw him at a distance, she ran out to meet him. She stopped the little procession of George, horse and sheep, took her son in her arms, held him, and sobbed.

"I was so worried, my son."

"It's okay, Mother. I am fine."

She sobbed one more time, sniffed, regained her composure, and said, "Where is your grandfather and William?"

"They are taking the two men to Chinle, to the hospital."

He explained what happened and finished with, "William and Grandfather are okay, but they will be back late."

She nodded. "Let's look at that lamb."

George led Nochero to the barn, while his mother placed the other sheep back in the pen, and then joined him.

George lifted the lamb off Nochero. He took it to the empty stall and set it down in a bed of hay. It cried softly, and George tried to soothe it.

His mother touched the lamb's back leg and the lamb cried out.

She bit her lip and shook her head.

"Can we fix it?" George asked.

"It's badly broken, George. I don't know."

"Can we try? Please?"

She looked at George doubtfully, saw the hurt, and hope in his eyes, and said, "I will try."

She asked George to get two small sticks from a pile of kindling in the corner of the barn, and then took the little handkerchief she had in her pocket and tore it into strips that she could use to bind the sticks to the lamb's leg.

Together, with George holding the lamb down, she straightened the crooked leg as best she could, and then put on the splint. The lamb cried, but settled down as George held it, pet it and spoke soothingly to it.

"It's the best we can do. We'll see in the morning."

George nodded without looking at her.

"Go get yourself cleaned up and then go to bed."

George looked up at her with tears in his eyes. "I would like to sleep in the barn tonight with her and Nochero." And then said, "If that is okay with you, Mother."

She smiled, kissed his forehead, embraced him and said, "Go change your underwear at least to something dry, and bring a blanket and a pillow. I will wait until you come back."

George set the lamb down gently, and then ran out of the barn to the house, changed out of his wet boxers into clean, dry ones. He grabbed his pillow from his bed, kissed Robert, who was sound asleep, took a light Navajo blanket that had been kicked off the bed, and ran back to the barn. He made a bed for himself in the stall next to the lamb that looked like it was asleep.

Nochero stood nearby, silent and strong, watching them.

George's mother went up to the big horse, gave him a hug and a pat and then to George said, "Yá'át'ééh," and "Goodnight, my son."

"Yá'át'ééh. Goodnight, Mother."

She left, closing the barn door behind her, leaving George in the dark.

With one hand gently on the lamb, George thought about the evening, about William and him wanting to leave, about Nochero, about the two men who stole the sheep and who ended up hurt and going to the hospital.

He wondered if what he had done disappointed his grandfather. All he had wanted to do was to get back the sheep, to protect them and his family. He hadn't meant to hurt them.

Saddled with a heavy heart, he shut his eyes, but only saw the wreck of the pickup truck, the little lamb with the broken leg, and he heard its cries.

He began to weep for the third time that evening. He decided he wasn't a very good Navajo, not worthy of the coming of age ceremony, and that he had so much to learn.

He shut his eyes to the sounds of the horses snorting and snuffling and shuffling in the barn. He tried to sleep, but it took a long time, and it wasn't very peaceful.

JOSEPH LEWIS 123

CHAPTER FORTY-SEVEN

Fishers, Indiana

It was Saturday, technically his day off, and when Brett said he needed to talk to him, Dominico drove forty minutes to Fishers from his house, on the north side of Indy. They sat at the kitchen table and Brett explained their suspicions that someone had been in the house not once, but twice. As he and Bobby had agreed and even though it was embarrassing, he laid out all the evidence.

"Guys, you think someone was in the house, at night, to look through your dirty laundry? Seriously, does that make any sense to you?"

Bobby looked at Brett, and defiantly, Brett said, "Yes, twice. He was in my basket twice and in Bobby's once. He dug through my underwear drawer and was in my closet. My bed wasn't made the way I normally make it, so I think he did something in my bed."

"You told me all that already, but guys, it just doesn't make any sense. There isn't any logic to it."

Brett folded his arms across his chest and glared at him.

"As a cop... a detective, I look for a motive."

Brett shrugged. "He's a pervert."

Dominico smiled sympathetically. "Guys, if it were anyone else, I would laugh in their face."

"Seriously?" Bobby asked.

"Seriously."

"There's no other explanation," Brett said.

Dominico leaned forward and took a gentle hold of Brett's forearm. "Let's look at the logic. Nothing was open except the sliding door in the family room that first night. Someone could have gone out at some point the night before or early in the morning. And whoever did that, could have simply forgotten to shut it tightly and lock it, right? You have to agree that it's a reasonable, logical explanation, right?"

Brett looked away from him and stared at his hands. He knew he had lost his argument.

"The second night, while everyone was in the house-"

"-asleep!"

Dominico nodded, and said, "Asleep... there were no doors or windows open. So, how could he have gotten in?"

Brett and Bobby stared at each other, neither willing to look at their uncle.

"Unless the guy's a magician or had a key, there is no way anyone could have gotten in."

Bobby glanced at Dominico and then back at Brett. Brett refused to look at Dominico.

"Right?"

Brett shrugged. Bobby nodded, and then blushed, feeling guilty for not backing up Brett.

Dominico got up, rummaged around in the refrigerator, found some lemonade, went to the cupboard, pulled out a glass and poured himself some. Then he leaned against the counter and stared at his nephews.

"You don't believe us, do you?" Brett asked.

He smiled at him. "I believe you believe it. It just doesn't seem plausible or logical to me."

"You're not going to tell mom or dad, are you?" Bobby asked.

"Of course not."

The relief was visible on both boys' faces.

"But guys, socks, really? That's so old. I think every guy in the world beats off and used his socks at your age. Hell, I used my socks when I was your age and I'm willing to bet your dad did too."

"Oh man! That's so gross!" Brett said. "I don't want to know if you or dad, oh my God! That's so gross!" he said with disgust.

"That's such a gross picture in my head!" Bobby laughed.

"Hey, I'm just sayin'," Dominico said with a laugh.

Brett got up, went to the refrigerator, took out a bottle of water, unscrewed the cap and drank some.

Dominico set his glass down on the counter, went over to Brett, hugged him and kissed his forehead. "We still buddies?"

"Yeah," he answered hugging him back.

Dominico kissed him again and held his face in both of his hands. "Just in case, you and Bobby should be careful. Make sure the windows and doors are locked before you go to bed. Okay?"

"Yeah."

"And, be careful about what adults you spend time with."

Brett's expression changed and Dominico noticed.

"What?"

Brett shrugged and said, "Last night, I went to the Pacers' game with Austin and Coach Coleman."

Dominico let go of Brett, took a step back and stared at him.

"Wait! You're worried about some guy breaking into your house, digging around in your dirty laundry, and you didn't think it could be somebody like Coleman? A single guy who hangs around with kids?"

"Coach wouldn't do that! He's taken me to stuff before!"

"And you don't find that a bit odd? Some guy who's three times your age, a single guy, who hangs around with kids?"

"He doesn't hang around with kids! He's taken me to one basketball game, maybe a movie. He's also taken me to three track meets in Chicago and St. Louis. He doesn't do anything to me!"

"Except, just maybe, come into the house at night while you're sleeping and dig around looking for your socks and underwear."

"Wait," Bobby said. "You said you didn't think anyone was in the house."

Dominico took a deep breath. "Guys, I just want you to be careful. And hanging out with some dude who's three times your age isn't being careful."

"Coach Coleman is my friend! He's a good guy and he wouldn't do anything to me!"

Brett stormed out of the room not willing to talk about it any further, especially to his uncle. But he wondered about his coach. And he didn't want to think that his coach would ever do something like that.

CHAPTER FORTY-EIGHT

Fishers, Indiana

He liked being with Brett, though he would have preferred he was with him and him alone. It couldn't be helped, however, at least not yet.

He had a plan, a good plan. It was almost fully fleshed out.

A nice pun: fleshed. He chuckled at his wit.

Anyway, he had a plan and he was close to putting it in play. He thought it was almost foolproof. Scratch that, it was foolproof. He'd be alone with Brett, and they would enjoy each other. He was sure of that.

But because he was exceptional at planning, he also had a contingency and had lofted a proposal that was being considered. However, he didn't want to consider the contingency, at least not yet. So, he shoved that out of his mind and focused on his plan.

Timing was everything and he had to make sure, to make absolutely certain it would be just the two of them and no one else to disturb them.

That thought grew larger and clearer with each passing day, each passing hour, and each passing minute. He thought of Brett as much as he did fine food. After all, in a basic way, Brett was a kind of food, or at least he would be. Soon.

It was the thought of Brett, his beauty, his eyes, his smile, his body.

Oh, he could barely contain himself.

Clever of him to think of that word, another nice pun. He was on a roll. Two clever puns.

He was on his mark. All he needed was somebody to say, "Get set" and then "Go!"

He chuckled at that thought. Damn, he was clever, smart and good-looking. Scratch that. He was hot.

He couldn't wait. He could barely wait to see Brett, all of Brett. Yes, he could barely wait.

And he chuckled again. He was so clever.

CHAPTER FORTY-NINE

East of Round Rock, Navajo Indian Reservation, Arizona

George woke, panting, stiff, and sweaty. It was hot and stuffy in the barn and at some point, he must have kicked off the blanket. Even though the open door splashed in a little light, it was still pretty dark, and he didn't know what time it was.

He stretched, yawned and tried to piece together the dream.

In it, there was a man trying to kill him. No, several men. All of them were *biligaana*. In his dream, George wasn't afraid. Rather, he had accepted it as fact and knew this was what he was supposed to do. He was supposed to protect someone. No, more than one, and they were *biligaana*, too. *Biligaana*, but not *biligaana* at the same time. He was no longer living with his family, with is mother, his brothers and his sister. He was no longer living with his grandmother or grandfather. This made him sad. His grandfather was near, but wasn't, and George had no idea what that meant.

The Navajo believed that dreams were spiritual and not to be taken lightly. His grandfather talked to him many times about dreams, and spirits and the spiritual world. He taught him that the spiritual world was as real as the world in which he existed, the world in which he walked and talked.

George frowned. The dream didn't make sense and as he had done so often, especially lately, he would have to ask his grandfather to help him make sense of it.

The other troubling dream, though it was exciting, was about Rebecca. He had several lately and they always ended up the same way. Messy and sticky, and very much like what happened when he was with Rebecca. In fact, his dreams about Rebecca were variations of what had happened when he was with Rebecca.

He had health class and knew about sex and the changes that would take place, but somehow, he must have been daydreaming when they talked about these kinds of dreams.

He yawned again and noticed that he was sticking out of the fly in his boxers and he felt himself. He waited for it to grow soft, but because he kept remembering his dream and Rebecca and her soft bronze breasts and what she had done to him, it wasn't getting softer. If anything, it grew harder and he considered using his hand, something he seldom did. It was only recently that he had begun experimenting with that, especially after the experience with Rebecca. But he resisted, because he was concerned that someone might come into the barn and catch him.

So instead, he stood up and adjusted his boxers so nothing poked out the opening and he hoped it would grow softer soon.

And that was when he remembered why he had slept in the barn. He searched the stall, and then the barn, but the little lamb with the broken leg was gone.

CHAPTER FIFTY

Washington, D.C.

Pete and Summer were frustrated and tired, and the jet lag didn't help. Chet was, well, Chet. It was hard for either of them to tell what he was feeling at any given moment.

And the atmosphere in the conference room was tense. Another dead body, another fourteen-year-old boy, found in the same state that an eleven-year-old boy was taken from. It seemed to confirm Chet's theory, at least in Pete's and Summer's mind. Logan felt otherwise, and Douglas played Switzerland and didn't commit to one side or the other.

Worst of all, other than one more dead boy and one boy taken, there was no other news, and no other leads.

There were no more questions and there wasn't anything more to discuss, so Musgrave quit shuffling papers and looked up, his eyes fixed on Pete.

"Who did you contact?"

Pete frowned at him, feigning ignorance. "What?"

"You must have made a phone call. I want to know who you called."

Summer looked from Musgrave to Pete, trying to anticipate Pete's response. Chet shook his head, turned off his laptop, and pushed it away from him.

"I don't really know what you mean," Pete said innocently.

"Someone called in Rapid Response. It wasn't me. You don't have that kind of clout. They had already turned down Storm. Whoever you called, and I know it was you who made a call, told them to get moving. I want to know who you contacted."

"Well, Logan, I actually made a couple of calls. This morning, I called my mother. She's old and has Alzheimer's and didn't remember me, but we had a nice conversation."

Musgrave leaned forward and jabbed a finger at him. "You're pushing it."

"And I rearranged a dental and eye appointment, but I doubt if either one called Rapid Response."

Musgrave stood up, leaned over the table and shouted, "I want to know who you called!"

Pete kept a smile on his face, spoke quietly and said, "I might have made a couple of other calls, but it's been a busy day and I can't remember them all. You know, I was out in the field investigating the murder of a fourteen-year-old boy and the kidnapping of an eleven-year-old boy."

"You insubordinate ass!"

"Speaking of asses, I wasn't sitting on mine in a cushy chair, in an air-conditioned office, shuffling papers and picking up some paper cuts in the process."

Logan Musgrave's face turned from red to almost purple. The veins stuck out in his neck. "I'm suspending you, indefinitely."

Pete shrugged, puffed up his cheeks and then sighed, and shrugged again.

"Whatever you say, Chief. I don't mind taking a couple of days off. I'm sure Summer and Chet can pick up the load."

"Guys, can we—"

Musgrave pointed a finger at Summer, cutting her off.

"But then again, I suppose I could make another phone call like the one you suggest I did, and who knows, the suspension might get lifted, and what would that mean for you and me and the team?"

Musgrave kicked his chair into the wall with a thud, picked up his papers, and glared at Kelliher. His jaw was so tight Chet wondered absently if someone could break their teeth that way.

"Don't call me until you actually have a lead. Otherwise, you're wasting my time."

He put his hand on the door knob and before he walked out the door, Pete said, "So Chief, how many days would you like me to take off?"

"Fuck you, Kelliher. Fuck you!"

JOSEPH LEWIS 131

CHAPTER FIFTY-ONE

Arlington, Virginia
"Kelliher is smarter and better than we thought."

The man on the other end of the phone was silent, waiting for either more information or a recommendation. After all, he paid him handsomely for both.

"For the most part, he and Storm linked the dump sites with the pickups. I think we need to lay low for a while. Or if you decide you need more... ponies, then I think you need to shop in a different area of the country."

The man on the other end of the phone sighed audibly.

"I'm a businessman. I have a thriving business, because I provide a product that patrons demand. I provide ponies to those who have a craving for them. It's simply supply and demand."

He turned around slowly, casually, and searched the street for anyone who might be paying too much attention to him. Or perhaps, someone who might be trying too hard to seem like he or she wasn't paying any attention to him.

No one; at least on casual glance, and no one sitting in a car, reading a map, or staring at him, either.

"I understand supply and demand. I just think it would be wise to lay low or shop in a different part of the country."

The man sighed again and said, "I'm not done shopping yet, and the Midwest is such a fertile ground. Innocent, wholesome. I have a lead on a pony in Wisconsin and I've had an inquiry about a possible pick up of a brown-haired pony in Indiana in exchange for services. I've seen pictures and both ponies are intriguing. Beautiful ponies. Powerful, athletic."

"Wisconsin and Indiana are too close. I mean, for God's sake. We were just in Ohio, Michigan and Minnesota. So, maybe out go out west or perhaps further south."

"I could do that, but then transport becomes difficult, expensive, and risky. Those are three words a good businessman never wants to hear. I certainly don't want to hear them."

"Dammit, you pay me to advise you!" He raised his voice, so he turned around in a slow one-eighty, concerned that someone might have overheard him.

But there was no one within ten yards of him on the somewhat sleepy and slow side of the street, perpendicular to the busy downtown.

"I also pay you for protection. To protect me and my business, not to mention our patrons."

In a quieter voice, he said, "And if you're not willing to listen to me, I can't protect you or your business."

"You mean, protect *us* and *our* business."

"Fine! *Us* and *our* business," he hissed through his teeth.

The man laughed humorlessly. "Yes, *us* and *our* business, for which I pay you handsomely."

This man was infuriating, egotistical, and arrogant beyond belief and unwilling to listen to any reason whatsoever. If he could cut his losses and walk away, he would, but he knew he couldn't. He was in too deep, far too deep.

He finally gave up and asked, "So, what are you going to do?"

The man laughed. "I'm going to send them shopping for a pony. That's what I'm going to do."

He heard the man sip something, because he thought he heard ice clink in a glass.

"After all, I'm a businessman who understands supply and demand."

And the phone call evidently ended, because he was left listening to dead air. He turned off his cell, slipped it into his pocket, swore softly, and walked down the street to his car.

CHAPTER FIFTY-TWO

East of Round Rock, Navajo Indian Reservation, Arizona

George decided that Nochero wasn't all that wild, because not only did he ride the stallion bareback the night before, he was able to trim the horse's hooves, tack on horseshoes, trim his mane and tail, and bathe and brush him. And, without any fuss at all, Nochero allowed George to give him a bridle, a saddle blanket, and a saddle. Nochero had to have had experience with all of this in a different lifetime.

George rode Nochero easily. The big horse seemed to know what George wanted, where he wanted to go, and how best to get there. Of course, a handful of oats, a little hay, a couple of carrots and an apple or two certainly helped the friendship grow.

The heat of the day was stifling, especially after the storm the night before, but George loved the look and feel of the desert after a good hard rain. If it was possible, George sat a little taller and a little straighter on top of Nochero, staring out over the pasture where the sheep grazed. Finally, he dismounted, looped the reins over the saddle horn and let Nochero graze with the sheep.

"Yá'át'ééh," George said in greeting to his grandfather.

His grandfather smiled and answered, "Yá'át'ééh."

George sat down next to his grandfather, took off his straw cowboy hat and wiped his brow with the back of his hand, and then replaced his hat.

His grandfather looked out over the pasture. "I missed saying my morning prayers with you."

George pulled his knees up to his chest, stared straight ahead, and answered, "I said mine before I cleaned up and took care of Nochero."

His grandfather smiled and nodded, pleased that George followed the traditional Navajo way, and never doubting that George had done what he had said he did. He knew his grandson was honest.

They sat together in silence, watching the sheep and Nochero, and then his grandfather said, "There is trust between you and Nochero."

George nodded. "Do you think I can keep him?"

"I believe that is up to Nochero," he paused and smiled, "He is content."

George stared at the black stallion, who turned to look back at the two of them, and then went back to grazing.

"My grandson has something on his mind?"

George stared at the ground and then out at the sheep, and then said without looking at him, "Grandfather, are you disappointed in me?"

"Why would I be disappointed in my grandson?"

George wiped tears out of his eyes and said, "Those two men were hurt because of me. They crashed their pick up because of me. The lamb broke its leg and mother had to kill it because it was in pain. I've been crying a lot and I don't know what's wrong with me."

His grandfather nodded, but didn't say anything.

"So, Grandfather, are you… disappointed in me?"

His grandfather looked at him without expression. "Why did you chase after them?"

"Because they came onto our land and stole two of our sheep, and I wanted to protect our land and our sheep."

"Your intentions were right and just. You acted, not of yourself, but of your family. That is right and just. There was no malice in your intention."

George sensed a, *but* was coming and his grandfather didn't disappoint him.

"What is greater, the life of a lamb or the life of a man?"

Without hesitation, George said, "The life of a man."

"But life is life. All life is important," he reached down into the sand and picked up several ants, "From the smallest ant to Nochero' from a lamb to a man. All life is important."

Confused, George said, "I do not understand, Grandfather."

"You defended your family. You acted to protect and rescue the sheep. That is right and just," he stopped, looked at George and said, "All life is sacred. One of Mother Earth's creatures is no greater or less than any other. You must ask yourself, what is in your heart? That is the question you must ask."

Tears sprung to his eyes and George said, "I was angry that they came onto our land and took our sheep. I wanted to get the sheep back."

"You acted not of yourself, but for them. You acted to protect life."

"But I hurt the two men and ended up hurting the lamb."

"Your intention was right and just. Sometimes our actions might hurt others even though we do not mean for that to happen."

"So, was I wrong?"

JOSEPH LEWIS 135

"There was no malice in your intentions. You acted to protect."

George was confused. He knew that his grandfather was trying to teach him a lesson but he didn't understand it, so he sat in silence.

"My grandson has something else on his mind?"

"Grandfather, why am I crying all the time? I never used to do that."

"You will have a coming of age ceremony in a few days. At that time, you will be considered a man. Your heart and your soul are responding to nature as all of life does. There is nothing wrong with tears. Tears are a sign of what is in your heart and soul. Just as your body bleeds, so does your heart and soul."

"But you said that good Navajos do not show their emotion."

"But when your heart and soul speak, it is important to give them their voice, he smiled, gave George a gentle elbow and said, "And your body is waking up and having special dreams."

George blushed. "Yes, I have dreams."

"About a pretty girl, I'm sure."

George nodded. "I never used to have those kinds of dreams."

His grandfather laughed, but not at George, and said, "Grandson, if your body and your heart and your soul and the spirits have something to say, they will speak. Your dreams are normal. All men, *Dine'* and *biligaana* have them. It is a sign that you are becoming a man. It is nothing to be frightened of. It is nothing to be ashamed of."

"But these dreams are messy and I sleep in the same bed with Robert and William."

"Messy or not, you are becoming a man. It is natural to have these dreams."

George nodded and remained silent.

"My grandson has something else on his mind other than pretty girls and tears."

"Grandfather, after I had... that dream, I had a different dream, and I don't understand it." He told his grandfather about the dream without skipping any details, and finished with, "I don't know what it means."

His grandfather took out his pipe, loaded it with tobacco and lit it up, and then offered it to George, who said, "No thank you," as he did each time his grandfather offered him the pipe.

"I had a dream. Several times I have had that dream, and spirits are speaking to me. In it, you are brave and stand to protect others, men and boys with hearts of *Dine'* though they are *biligaana*. They are your brothers, but not your brothers. You fight bravely, even though it is dangerous. I was proud."

Puzzled, George wondered why his grandfather hadn't shared this dream with him before, and who were these boys who were his brothers?

"In time, you will have a choice to make, in time, a difficult choice. It will be dangerous. It will be a choice that a man, not a boy, should make. But the spirits are telling both of us that in time, you will have to make a choice."

"What kind of choice, Grandfather?"

His grandfather waved his hand in dismissal and then said gently, "This I do not know. Only the spirits know and when the time is right, you will know, because the spirits will tell you."

George nodded, though he didn't understand. In fact, it worried him.

"Do not be troubled, my Grandson. You and I have time to prepare."

"But, Grandfather," George didn't know how he wanted to say it, so he said it as best he could, "Grandfather, in my dream... what did it mean that you were there, but not there? Why wasn't mother there? Why weren't my brothers and sister and grandmother there?"

His grandfather shook his head. "These things I do not know. In time, maybe, we will understand. But my Grandson, you cannot trouble yourself too greatly over what the spirits tell you or do not tell you. They speak in their own time and in their own way."

George frowned, wishing he was smarter. He was patient, very patient, yet there were some things that went above even his patience level.

"My Grandson, go to my saddlebag and bring out a gift I have for you."

George got up, walked through the stand of pines to the roan that his grandfather preferred to ride, reached into the saddlebag and found a bag of jerky, and wondered if that was the gift his grandfather might have for him. To be certain, he left it there, and went to the other side, reached in and lifted out a beautiful knife and sheath.

The blade was shiny and sharp. The shaft was eight inches long and the handle was an extra four inches, and made of elk bone bound to the shaft with leather. It had balance and heft and fit his hand much like it was naturally made for it. George had never seen it before and knew it was the gift his grandfather spoke of.

He carried it back to his grandfather and offered it to him, but his grandfather smiled, waved it away and nodded.

George held it gently and admired its beauty.

"I planned to give this to you on the day you come of age. I believe we are close enough to your ceremony. Because of our dreams, I believe it should become yours now."

"It is beautiful, Grandfather. Thank you."

"You and I will practice each morning before we say our prayers. It needs to be one and part of your hand, each hand. It needs to be one with your right hand and your left hand, just as your thumb and your finger are one and part of your right hand and your left hand. You and I will practice."

George took it, smiled at his grandfather, who smiled back, nodded and then puffed on his pipe. Puffing on his pipe was a signal that for the time being, there weren't any more words to share between them.

CHAPTER FIFTY-THREE

Fishers, Indiana

The banquet in the middle school cafeteria the Thursday before Memorial Weekend was the official end of the school track season. It was the harbinger of the end of the school year, and the beginning of summer. Brett might have gotten used to the idea that Da'Shawn Grimes had been murdered, but he hadn't gotten over it, and he certainly hadn't forgotten. As his uncle had suggested, Brett used permanent marker to put a DG on both of his track shoes in honor of the murdered boy. He hadn't lost a one hundred or a two hundred or a long jump since that meet, and he had earned a PR in each of those meets.

He received the MVP plaque, which was unusual for a fifth grader, but then, there hadn't been anyone on the team anywhere near the number of points Brett had earned.

At the end of the banquet, and after most everything had been cleaned up, there were only a few parents and a few of the kids left. Coach Coleman walked over to Thomas and Victoria McGovern.

"Can I speak to you for a minute?"

Thomas was a popular English professor at Butler University who tended to be on the quiet side. He was medium built and handsome with light brown hair. In terms of personality, Bobby had taken after him more so than Brett, but both boys shared the stubbornness and bull-headed determination that both parents had. Victoria, a surgical nurse at St. Vincent's Heart Center, had long dark hair and moved like an athlete. It was from her that both boys got their darker complexion and chestnut brown hair with matching eyes. Brett's personality was more like his mother's, and the two of them were quite close, while Bobby and his father shared that same closeness, especially since both liked to write as well as read.

They all sat down at the table with the fewest crumbs. Coleman swept them off and onto the floor with his hand and then pulled out some registration forms.

"With your permission, I'd like to enter Brett into a couple of summer invitationals. Three of them are the same as the ones he ran in last summer, two in Chicago and one in St. Louis. But there is a big meet in Pennsylvania, called the Hershey Invite that has a national reputation, and I think there will definitely be some college coaches there. St. Louis and one of the Chicago meets are coming up in June. And the other Chicago meet and the Hershey Invite are in July.

"I don't know what your plans are for the summer, and I know it's quite a time commitment, but the St. Louis meet is a nice family meet and there are a lot of things to do there. And Hershey is an even better venue. I thought I'd just toss these ideas out there for you to think about."

"It would be nice to take a family vacation," Vicky said.

"And if you can't work it into your schedule, I'm willing to take Brett and a friend or Bobby to whatever meets you can't go to. Why don't you think about it and let me know. There are due dates on the registrations and the first due date comes up in a week."

Under normal circumstances, Brett would have pushed and pulled his mom and dad right then and there to let him compete with or without them coming along. After all, Coach Coleman had taken him to two meets last summer where he got noticed by a couple of college coaches and where he earned his first national time. But ever since his uncle had yelled at him and Bobby that Saturday in the kitchen, he had rebuffed his coach for a movie and an arena football game, as well as a lake trip with some of Brett's friends. Even though his friends went, he didn't.

"I'd like to go to them if I can," Brett finally said. "I mean, if it's alright with you," he added looking at his parents, "If not all of them, maybe two or three of them, at least?"

"We'll talk about it and let you know soon," Thomas said to Coleman as he shook his hand.

As their conversation broke up, Brett approached Coleman, stuck out his hand and said, "Coach, thank you for helping me this year. I appreciate it."

Coleman smiled at him, placed a hand on his shoulder and said, "I didn't do much, Brett. You have the drive and intensity and that's half the battle. All I did was tweak your form. You did the rest."

Brett smiled. "Well, thanks, Coach."

"If you stop in and see me tomorrow sometime, I'll have some summer workouts for you."

"Okay, thanks!"

As they left the cafeteria, Bobby fell in step with Brett and said quietly so that no one else heard, "What about what Uncle Tony said?"

Brett frowned. "Some of my other friends do things with him and he hasn't done anything to them. If nothing happens to them, nothing will happen to me. Besides, I like him. I trust him."

Bobby nodded. "I'll go with you if you want... I mean, if one of your friends can't go."

"Maybe," Brett said, already thinking ahead that Austin would be more fun to be with.

CHAPTER FIFTY-FOUR

East of Round Rock, Navajo Indian Reservation, Arizona

It was early morning and still quite dark. The desert and mesa smelled of sage and something earthy. An owl hooted off in the distance. Nearer, a coyote howled at the moon that still hung low and pale in the sky. Nochero and the roan stood just down the main path.

George mirrored his grandfather's hand, arm, foot and leg movements, shifting the knife from one hand to the other. Dressed only in a traditional soft leather breechcloth that hung to his mid-thigh, he had a sheen of sweat covering his face, his chest, his back, his arms, and his legs, having been at this for the better part of thirty minutes. Each morning for the past several weeks, the routine was the same, and George was now able to anticipate the next moves based upon the previous ones. He focused on and controlled his breathing, in through his nose and out through his mouth, no longer intent on the act, but doing it naturally. In his grandfather's words, the knife had become one with George's hands, both the left and the right, his movements guided by the spirits.

The moon disappeared, the morning had begun to lighten, and the beginnings of a warm red sunrise peeked over the rim of the mesa, a short ride to the east of their ranch, towards the Chuska Mountains. That was their sign to stop their knife exercises and begin their prayers to Father Sun.

This was no normal day. This was George's birthday, and the day of his coming of age ceremony. While he concentrated on his prayers, in the back of his mind were the songs he practiced and had learned in anticipation of this special day.

When the sun was fully up over the rim and shining on them, they finished their prayers, and his grandfather signaled to him to begin his songs.

George performed as his grandfather expected him to, his voice clear, his words in his native Navajo language true. The songs were beautiful in their own simple, primitive way. He knew his ancestors would be proud and he hoped his grandfather would be too.

When he finished, he turned to face his grandfather, who stood with his hands behind his back, his eyes shut, and his faced tilted slightly up. Knowing not to disturb him, George waited patiently, content to look over the valley below them at a herd of six elk. There was at least one good-sized bull and two young calves among them.

"My grandson, I am proud of you."

"Thank you, Grandfather."

He smiled at George, nodded and said, "Your ceremonial name is Shadow."

George thought about it, unsure why his grandfather had given him that name, but he did not betray his feelings.

"The shadow is silent, but present everywhere one chooses to look. The shadow is present in sunlight and in darkness. It advances before and follows after. It stands with the strong and the weak, with man and animal, with tree and rock."

George's eyes and his smile betrayed his feelings, proud of the name his grandfather had given him.

"Thank you, Grandfather."

His grandfather nodded and then sat on a flat rock, patting a rock to his side, indicating that George should sit with him.

"There were two paths up this mesa. The one you took, the harder of the two, few people know, certainly no *biligaana*," he paused to let that sink in, and then said, "What did you learn from taking that path, Shadow?"

George thought about the question before he answered. Finally, he said, "There are two paths. Both lead to the top. One is easy and one is hard."

"And what does that mean?"

George's face clouded in thought. "I took the path that was harder. I had to watch my footing, because the path wasn't clear. I had to climb over rocks. There were thorns. I scraped my shin. There were places where I had to guess where to walk. The path you took is the path we usually take. It is easy to see the path. We don't have to climb over rocks. There is sand and we see our footprints and the tracks from other creatures as we walk on it."

"All that is true, my grandson," his grandfather said nodding.

George was patient and remained quiet as he waited for his grandfather to speak further.

"Shadow, there are those who choose the easy path in life. There are those who take the harder path. Sometimes we choose the path we take. Sometimes the path is chosen for us," he turned to face George, looked at him solemnly and said, "Shadow, I believe that each of us takes different kinds of paths through life, both easy and hard. I believe we choose the path we take," he paused, nodded, and continued, "I believe you will be faced with a path that is not of your choosing. It will be difficult. It will be hard. But there will be those with the heart of *Dine'* to help and guide you on this path."

Puzzled, George asked, "Who, Grandfather? And where will you and grandmother, mother and my brothers and sister be?"

George's grandfather waved his hand. "Shadow, your ancestors, the *Dine'* will always be with you."

George realized his grandfather did not answer his question, and the good feeling he had about his Coming of Age Ceremony left him as one would exhale a breath. Despite the warmth of the sun, George shivered.

CHAPTER FIFTY-FIVE

Washington, D.C.

It was steamy hot and humid in D.C. It was muggy and tough to breathe as if one wore a warm wet blanket. It was on days like this the city had an unpleasant combination of smells, featuring that of unwashed flesh and wet dog.

Summer had never gotten used to it. Nebraska smelled of mowed lawn, freshly cut hay, and of well-kept beef cattle. Wind blows at an almost constant twenty knots, which makes walking or running challenging, but Summer had done both. She loved the state, the folksiness of it, the simple and uncomplicated life that was lived there. The pace was slow, unmeasured, and she missed it, compared to the constant traffic, the noise and rudeness of D.C. D.C. wasn't clean. D.C. was messy and dirty and complicated by politics and intrigue, neither of which she had any interest in or passion for.

After that first meeting with Thatcher Davis, Summer received an email from him, just to thank her for taking the time to meet with him, and then another asking her to lunch. She had never responded to the first and declined the second, begging off because she didn't have time.

But the fact was, she did have time, lots of time. A frustrating amount of time, actually, because she, Pete and Chet had run out of ideas. They had nothing.

They checked out pedophiles on the database in each state where a body was found and either personally interviewed each, or had local authorities interview them. Chet set up a system that let him know whenever an Amber Alert was broadcast, to see if there were any matches to kids they found. Out of sixteen alerts for boys, there were nine boys in the same age range, and who seemed to fit the profile: white, athletic, a leader, an intact family with at least one sibling.

But there was nothing else.

Nothing.

Taking a chance and remembering Davis' offer to be an objective set of eyes, she called him and asked if he'd like to do lunch. She was thinking of a deli that had a great roast beef sandwich with a side of coleslaw. Instead, he took her to Four Seasons because, as he explained it, he liked the ambiance of the place, and because of that statement, she considered for a second time that he might be gay, divorced or not.

Finished with her almond chicken salad, and munching on a breadstick and still wishing for a roast beef sandwich lathered with horseradish, Summer asked, "Why did you join the FBI?"

"Seemed like the thing to do at the time," and then he laughed dryly.

"But you could have practiced any kind of law, anywhere you wanted. Why here?"

He considered the question, rested his elbows on the table and rested his chin on his hands. "I was young and had only a vague plan after I had graduated. Honestly, I couldn't decide between corporate or criminal law. I decided both were similar, and joining the FBI gave me an opportunity for a steady income at a leisurely pace with interesting cases."

"Interesting cases?" Summer asked doubtfully.

"Well, think of Ruby Ridge, the Branch Davidians in Waco, The Pine Ridge mess in South Dakota. All of that had to be sorted out and... *handled* with the least amount of blowback to the FBI."

Amazed and interested, Summer asked, "You worked on those?"

"In one aspect or another." He shifted his head from one side to the other and added, "Sometimes in the middle of it, sometimes after the fact."

She found a new respect for Davis. Those were some of the biggest cases, and some of the worst messes the FBI had been involved with. To say he had a hand in it was something, she had to admit.

With a laugh, he said, "And you could have the same fun if you join my division."

"No, I like where I am, working with the people I work with."

"Even Kelliher?"

"*Especially* Kelliher."

"Tell me about him... from your vantage point."

"Pete's an old-time cop. He's part John Wayne and part Leroy Jethro Gibbs on *NCIS*. He's a great cop and an even better person. He never gives up. He has your back and he's honest and sincere. He cares."

"Impressive qualities."

"He's a good man."

Davis took a sip of ice water and peered at her over the rim. He set it down, wiped the corners of his mouth with the cloth napkin and said, "So. What can I do for you?"

Summer pushed her plate to the side and folded her hands in front of her. "We've hit dead end after dead end. We know what's happening, but we don't know by whom. We don't know when, but we know why."

Davis shut his eyes and nodded, thought for a minute or two, sipped his ice water and dabbed at his mouth with the cloth napkin.

"Sounds like you have a lot of holes. I don't understand how you know what's happening and why it's happening. I don't understand how you can know those two parts of the puzzle without knowing who or when."

"We know... we believe... it's a sex ring. Human trafficking. We know from the uniformity of the ages of the victims we've found and the consistency of the profiles of the victims, that we're dealing with age and sex specific pedophiles. We even believe when a body is found, that a child will end up missing from that same state."

"Impressive work Agent Storm, very impressive. What are your next steps?"

"That's just it. We don't have any next steps. None. Zip. Zero. Right now, we're just sitting around, waiting for the next boy to be found."

"Hmmm... that's depressing."

"Tell me about it."

"I'll tell you what. I'll give it some thought, make a few phone calls and see what I can find. In exchange, please consider my offer. Just consider it with an open mind."

"I have been thinking about it. Really, I have. I'm just not ready for it. I like what I do right now."

Davis smiled. "Okay. I'll still make a few calls and I'll still give it some thought. Give me a couple of days and I'll give you a call."

"Thank you. I appreciate it."

She turned around and looked for their waiter, but Davis said, "This is on me. I make more money than you do, and it has been my pleasure to have lunch with you today. I hope we can do this again."

Summer smiled and decided that she liked him. He was stately, charming, and had a dash of Cary Grant about him.

"I'd like that very much, thank you."

"The pleasure is all mine," Davis said with a smile.

CHAPTER FIFTY-SIX

Fishers, Indiana
Even though Brett loved football and basketball, summer was his favorite time of year. He liked the warmth, the sun, and just kicking back barefoot dressed in a pair of shorts. He and his friends rode their bikes to the local pool and would swim most of the day, or they'd ride their bikes to the middle school to play pickup basketball games. At night, they'd go to movies, have sleep-overs, and stay up late watching movies or playing video games or Wii.

And because his parents worked, he and Bobby had a lot of free, unstructured and unsupervised time, and that was the cherry on top of the sundae. Not that either boy did anything to warrant supervision or anything that would abuse their parents' trust, they just enjoyed the freedom that other kids their ages didn't have.

June flew by and so did half of July.

Deciding that three track meets instead of four were enough, Brett did very well in the St. Louis Track and Field Invitational, earning a PR and finishing third in the one hundred, and earning a PR in the two hundred, where he finished second. He didn't do as well in the long jump as he would have liked, only finishing eighth, but it was still a good trip. His mother took vacation time and drove both boys, along with Brett's friend, Austin, and Bobby's friend, Zach. hey spent time at the Zoo, and at a huge Six Flags, in Eureka, a southern suburb of St. Louis, before heading home.

Coleman took Brett and Austin to Chicago, where Brett finished second in the one hundred, third in the two hundred, earning PRs in both events; and second in the long jump, where he bettered his original PR by four inches. They booked two rooms, one for Coleman and one for the boys, and spent time at Taste of Chicago on the lakefront and lounging around the motel swimming pool, and the motel arcade.

But Brett and Bobby were looking forward to the Hershey Invite. Thomas and Vicky planned a leisurely family trip that would include the amusement park and Amish country, in addition to Brett's track meet. Coleman planned to travel separately and meet them there, and then head back right after the meet.

Several times over the weeks, Tony Dominico warned Brett about being too friendly with Coleman, but Brett had all but ignored him, because Coleman hadn't done or said anything suspicious or anything to make him uncomfortable.

Dominico had driven both boys to Chicago to catch a Cubs game. They shared a room and spent time in the sauna and pool, and then before heading back home, visited the Navy Pier.

He asked them if they noticed any other break-ins, but neither boy found anything unusual and Brett, more than Bobby decided that there had to have been a logical explanation for all of it, feeling foolish for their worry. Brett was pretty quick to dismiss it, but Bobby wasn't.

The two boys sat at the kitchen table, eating breakfast, when Brett's cell buzzed. He looked at the caller ID, saw that it was Dominico and answered it.

"Hey, what's up?" Brett asked.

"I'm taking the day off and wanted to know if you wanted to go shooting with me."

Brett had gone several times and surprised both himself and his uncle with how accurate he was with a variety of handguns.

"Sure."

"Tell Bobby that I'll take him out next week, okay?"

"Okay." Brett glanced at Bobby who was scribbling in his notebook, seemingly not paying attention, though Brett was pretty sure he was. "I'll tell him."

"I'll pick you up in an hour or so. It's hot and humid, so dress appropriately. Maybe when we're done, we'll pick up Bobby, get lunch and go swimming, okay?"

"Sounds good."

• • •

Dominico carried a black garbage bag in one hand and his duffle bag in the other down to the river. Brett followed, carrying his uncle's gun case. In it were two handguns, a .45 that Brett knew had a hell of a kick, along with a Glock .9. He liked the power of the .45, but was more comfortable with the Glock.

It was hotter than hot and more than humid, so Brett had his shirt off, hanging on his shoulder. He wore a pair of older athletic shoes, because it was sometimes muddy at the river and he didn't want to ruin any of his good ones.

Dominico took off his shirt, took Brett's off his shoulder and stuffed them into his gym bag. Then he set up seven cans on various rocks on a low hanging tree limb.

He walked back to Brett, placed a hand on his bare chest, and gently moved him back another ten yards and said, "We're going to try some new games this time. You're getting better and better, and your aim and your concentration are excellent, so I'm going to do my best to distract you," he said.

Brett smiled, nodded, "Whatever. I'll still do better than you."

Dominico. "Oh, is that a challenge?"

"Yeah, I'll bet you lunch."

"You're on, Kid. Just remember. I'm going to do all I can to distract you."

For the first round, Brett was given ten seconds to memorize the locations of the tin cans, made up of mostly soda cans with a few beer cans thrown in, and then turn his back on them, while Dominico counted down three... two... one. Then Brett was to turn around and fire from left to right, one shot at each target. Dominico would tally up the hits and misses, and then he'd take his turn.

Brett stared at the cans and then turned his back on them. Dominico counted down, and when he reached one, Brett turned and fired. He missed the first can, but hit the rest. Six out of seven.

"Pretty good, Kid. Not perfect like I'm going to be, but pretty good."

"Yeah, yeah, yeah. We'll see," Brett answered with a laugh.

Brett put the cans he shot in a little pile to be picked up later, and then set up new cans. He chose a few smaller cans, including a Carnation Sweetened Condensed Milk can and a Campbell's Soup Can, and filled in the rest with soda and beer cans.

Brett used his uncle's watch, because he never wore one, and let his uncle stare at them for ten seconds, and then Dominico turned around. Brett counted down and on one Dominico spun around and hit ten for ten.

"Ha! I'm looking forward to that lunch, Kid!"

"I'll catch you this time," though Brett wasn't all that confident.

"Oo, do I detect a little doubt?"

"No," Brett said with a laugh.

"We'll see."

Dominico set up seven cans, not bothering to pick up the ones he hit, and then walked back to Brett.

He licked his lips nervously, and said, "Okay, now for a real test."

"What?"

"Brett, part of being a good shot is to be able to focus in spite of all the distractions around you. Your life and the life of your partner could depend on it."

Brett nodded.

"To focus and concentrate is key to any situation that involves guns, and being able to hit your target. I've seen good men shot and killed, because they lost their focus and their concentration. That's what we're going to work on in this round."

"How?"

Dominico smiled, stepped behind Brett and placed both of his arms around him, and kissed the top of his head.

Then, still holding him in a gentle hug, his hands on Brett's stomach, he said, "I'll give you ten seconds to memorize the targets. This time, instead of turning around and firing, you're going to turn around and I'm going to do everything I can to distract you."

"What are you going to do?"

Dominico hugged him a bit tighter, his hand lowering and brushing Brett's shorts. "Whatever I can to distract you. Whatever I do, you have to concentrate and focus."

Brett shifted his stance, because it was too hot to be hugged. In fact, he didn't like anyone, especially a guy hugging him, except his mother and father, his grandmother, and his aunts.

"From left to right, number the cans one through seven. Memorize where they are, and then turn around, and when you turn back, I'll call out a number and that's the one you have to shoot at. One shot for each number. Seven shots total."

"I can do that."

"Remember, focus and concentrate. No matter what I do, ignore it and concentrate on your target. It could be the difference between life and death. Okay?"

"Yes."

"No matter what I do, focus and concentrate."

"I got it," Brett said impatiently, already wondering what his uncle would do to distract him.

"Okay, memorize the cans, both the locations and their place in order from one to seven. I'll give you ten seconds starting... now."

Dominico still had his arms around Brett, his hands on Brett's stomach, one lingering low on his waist.

He let go, turned Brett around, and said, "Ready?"

Brett nodded, licked his lips, and nodded again.

"Okay, turn around, but don't shoot until I give you a number."

Brett turned around and Dominico immediately put his hands around Brett's waist, hugging him and gently tickling his stomach and ribs. Brett laughed and tried to step away.

"No, focus and concentrate, remember?"

Brett stood still, stifled a laugh and nodded.

"Number four."

Brett took aim and blew the Bud Lite can off the rock.

"Good. Focus and concentrate," Dominico said, as he kissed Brett's cheek.

Brett tried to turn away, and in a stern voice, Dominico said, "Focus, no matter what I do!"

"Well, don't be gross," Brett said nervously, trying to cover it up with a laugh.

Dominico poked him.

"Ouch!"

"Focus!" Dominico said through clenched teeth.

Brett nodded.

Dominico's hand traveled down Brett's stomach, lingered on his bellybutton, and then touched the front of his shorts, gripping him gently.

"Hey!" Brett said, trying to move away.

"Focus. Trust me, Brett. Just focus and concentrate. Number three."

Uncomfortable, not liking this game, Brett nonetheless focused on the soup can and blew it off the branch.

Dominico continued to hold onto him down there, squeezing and pulling it gently.

"Number one."

Brett hesitated, unsure of what he was going to do if his uncle continued touching him there.

"Trust me, Brett. I will never hurt you, I promise. Please trust me and above all, focus. Number one."

Again, Brett hesitated. He was fully hard, fully erect and his uncle held it firmly.

"Trust me, Brett, focus. Number one."

Brett took aim and missed high.

"Just trust me, Brett. I won't hurt you. Concentrate."

Brett stood still, not liking what his uncle was doing to him.

His uncle finally shifted his hand to Brett's stomach and Brett breathed a sigh of relief.

"Number four."

"I hit that one already."

"Oh yeah, sorry."

Brett noticed his uncle's breathing had changed. His mouth and breath were on Brett's right ear.

"Number two."

Brett took aim and hit the soda can off the low hanging branch.

"Good," Dominico said as he kissed Brett's cheek, near the corner of his mouth.

Dominico's hand dipped into Brett's shorts. His hand gripped him, then cupped him, and then gripped him and held on.

"Please stop. Don't do that."

"Trust me, Brett. Focus. Please. I won't hurt you, ever. Just focus."

"Stop," Brett said quietly, his voice just above a whisper. "Don't do that. Please, stop."

The gun was forgotten. No numbers were called. Dominico concentrated only on Brett, and Brett only on what his uncle was doing to him.

Brett lowered the gun and shut his eyes. He didn't like what his uncle was doing to him but he didn't know what to do.

And as his uncle pushed Brett's shorts and boxers down, and as he continued to do what Brett only did to himself in private and only occasionally, Brett was sickened with the thought that perhaps it was his uncle who had broken into their house that one night. In fact, he didn't have to break in, because his uncle had a key.

When Brett was finished, his uncle let go, and Brett didn't waste any time.

He threw the gun down, pulled up his boxers and shorts, and turned and ran, and didn't stop until he got home.

When he did get home a long time later, sweaty and tired, his uncle's car was already in the driveway and Dominico was leaning on the trunk waiting for him.

Dominico reached out, but Brett stormed past him, walked into the house and down the hall, not stopping when Bobby asked, "What's wrong?"

He got to his room, grabbed a clean pair of boxers and a clean pair of shorts and a t-shirt, went to the bathroom, shut and locked the door. He took as hot a shower as he could stand. He soaped up, rinsed, and then soaped up and rinsed again. Finally, he turned off the shower, placed his hands and his head against the back wall and tried to figure out what to do next.

If he said anything to his mother or father, they wouldn't believe him. After all, Dominico was his uncle. He didn't even know if Bobby would believe him. He thought of telling Coach Coleman, but then Coach would tell his parents and they still wouldn't believe him.

He didn't know what to do other than to tell no one and make sure he was never alone with his uncle again.

Ever again.

CHAPTER FIFTY-SEVEN

Arlington, Virginia
"You called?"

The man on the other end of the long-distance call said, "Yes. I would like an update."

He looked up and down the street, and then pretended to window shop, using the glass to scan the other side of the street. It didn't seem that any pedestrians were interested in him and he didn't see anyone in any parked cars.

"They found two more bodies. As I've said before, they've put together the dump sites with the pick-ups, but other than that, they have nothing. No leads. No threads. Nothing."

"I like the sound of that."

He heard something in the background, but couldn't make out what it was.

"Tell me, what about this Kelliher and Storm? What's happening with them?"

"Nothing, really. Kelliher is on a shit list, and Storm is on someone's short list. It's a matter of time before he's gone and she moves up. I think that's good on both counts."

"How does that help us?"

"Because, Kelliher means trouble for us. He's a damn good cop. He won't quit. He hasn't quit. And Storm, well, she's smart, a thinker. If she moves up, then we won't have to worry about her."

"I think that's very good news then. Thank you for your efforts."

He laughed dryly. "I haven't done all that much, because there isn't much to do."

The man on the other end laughed. "Well, keep doing that then."

And he laughed again and hung up.

CHAPTER FIFTY-EIGHT

Washington, D.C.
The three of them huddled in the conference room. Whether or not they had anything new, they had an agreement to meet once a week, because they didn't want the case to die, and they didn't want to forget about the kids who had been murdered and the kids who had been taken.

Since April, there were pictures of two more bodies posted on the wall, along with pushpins to mark where they had been found. Their families had been interviewed and their names recorded.

Two new pictures of fresh-faced, smiling boys, full of hope and full of dreams, both with futures bright and shiny. Not to be, however, because underneath those two pictures were two other pictures of the boys, dead. Pictures that showed their lives ended and cut short. Pictures that showed they died, naked and alone.

Nothing else new.

The most frustrating thing for Pete was doing nothing while waiting for another dead boy to be found. He wasn't built to sit on his ass and wait. He was built to find a lead, no matter how small and seemingly inconsequential. And then he'd pounce on it with both feet and beat it into submission until he had an answer.

Summer was the thinker of the three. She'd sit in near darkness, quiet and alone, and ponder and mull things over. While Pete wrote in his little notebook, Summer didn't take notes, but remembered even the smallest of details, especially names and places. Together, they would bounce things off of one another, usually with Summer asking the questions, while Pete positing theories and ideas.

Then, there was Chet. It was Chet who was fed the theories and ideas, and then he'd pound the keys to ether land and come up with a track to follow, some lead to chase.

But it was the end of August, three days before the first of September, and there was nothing.

Nothing.

CHAPTER FIFTY-NINE

East of Round Rock, Navajo Indian Reservation, Arizona
George noticed a difference in his less than talkative grandfather. Usually serious, he seemed more so, and George knew it was only a matter of time before his grandfather would share what he needed to, if he needed to.

As usual, knife exercises began his day, and with his confidence growing with each practice, George found himself moving at a quicker, smoother pace. Perhaps it was the sheer repetitive nature of the movements over the course of the summer that did it for him. Whatever it was, George found himself embellishing on the foot movements, and on his hand and arm actions, and reactions to the satisfied nod of approval from his grandfather. As the sun came up, he and his grandfather stood side by side, on the mesa, and greeted Father Sun, in prayer and song.

When they finished, they continued to stare at the land below, and at the Chuska Mountains in front of them. At least George did, because his grandfather had his eyes closed.

"Shadow, I believe it will come soon."

"What will come soon, Grandfather?"

The old man remained silent for a time and then still with his eyes closed, said, "I believe it will come to pass, the path you will walk."

Startled and uncomfortable, jolted back days ago to his conversation with his grandfather above the pasture as they sat and watched their sheep, George didn't know which question to ask first. *What path? When? What will happen to him and to his family, to his grandfather?*

"The spirits have shown me that you will be faced with choices. Each choice leads to another and so on."

"When, Grandfather?" George asked in a small voice.

His grandfather turned to him, smiled and placed a hand on his bare shoulder, and said, "There is time, Shadow. It is not today. It is not tomorrow. But the spirits tell me that you need to listen closely. You need to watch carefully."

George nodded solemnly.

JOSEPH LEWIS 157

"There are boys, *biligaana*, who are in danger. You will be drawn in, if you choose, to help them and they to help you. That is one path."

"And the other path?" George asked, not that he would ever shrink from doing what was right. His grandfather always taught him to help those in need, whether they were man or animal.

"The other path is to do nothing, to say nothing."

George shook his head, knowing that was not an option.

"It will not be very soon, but soon enough. You need to watch and listen," he tapped George's chest. "You must know your heart and trust that what you feel is true. Trust that your heart is *Dine'* and that it follows the way of the *Dine'.*"

George nodded solemnly.

"You and I have time. I know you want to ask when it shall come to pass and where it shall come to pass, but the spirits have not told me. When they do, it will be time. They have not done so."

Relieved, George sighed, and then said, "Grandfather, I do not know any boys who are *biligaana*."

His grandfather smiled. "In time."

CHAPTER SIXTY

Indianapolis, Indiana

Brett's cell buzzed.

He took it out of his pocket, read the caller ID, and shoved it back into his pocket. A minute or two later, it buzzed again, and he took it out of his pocket and read the text. It was a long one that left him shaking his head and sick to his stomach, so he deleted it without responding. This routine had been going on between the two of them for one and a half months, but because school would begin the day after Labor Day, in just three days, Brett would have less time to worry about him.

"Brett, can you come and get these?" his dad called from the backyard as he was piling hamburgers and hotdogs onto a plate.

"Yeah, yeah, yeah."

"Hustle or you won't get any," his dad teased.

He opened up the sliding door and pretended to move in slow motion, while his dad shook his head and tried not to laugh. Brett took the plate from his father, and again pretended to move backwards in slow motion and faked a stumble.

"You will eat whatever you drop," his dad cautioned with a laugh.

"I don't fumble. I never fumble. I've got great hands!"

"And you're rather full of yourself," his mother laughed.

Brett did a nifty spin move through the door opening, zigged left, zagged right, and placed the plate securely on the table, and then cheered for himself, arms up in the air and hopping up and down as if he had scored a touchdown.

"You're in a good mood," Victoria said.

"Football game next week and I'm starting both ways at halfback and safety."

"School starts on Tuesday," Bobby added with a smile.

"Don't ruin it for me, okay?"

"I like school."

Brett made a face. It wasn't like he hated it, but he couldn't say he liked it either.

His cell buzzed again and he ignored it.

"What does Austin want?" Tom asked coming through the door.

"Just football and school stuff," Brett lied. Then he noticed the extra place setting and asked, "Who's coming over?"

"I invited Tony," she went to the refrigerator, "Who wants what to drink?"

Brett barely heard her. He caught Bobby staring at him, but Brett ignored him.

"Bobby, why don't you sit on this side, and Tony and Brett can sit on that side?"

Brett was about to answer, but Bobby cut him off. "I'll sit with Brett on this side, that way Uncle Tony can have more room."

Not really caring one way or the other, Victoria said, "Okay, that works."

Brett looked at Bobby, who smiled at him. Brett nodded subtly at him.

. . .

Throughout the dinner, Brett answered his questions with one- or two- word answers and didn't comment on anything his uncle said. When his uncle asked if he and Bobby wanted to go to the Colts season opener, Bobby jumped at the opportunity, while Brett said that he preferred to watch it on TV, because he could see the replays, adding that Austin was having a whole bunch of friends over for a party.

"Are you sure, Brett? You love going to games," Tom said exchanging a look with his wife.

"Yeah," Brett answered and then to Tony, said, "Sorry."

"Can I still go?" Bobby asked.

"Sure. Tom, you want to go with us?"

"Yes, I'd love to, thank you."

And that was how it went ever since that day at the river in mid-July. Any and every offer by Dominico was rebuffed by Brett with a less than flimsy excuse. Brett didn't answer his calls. Brett never responded to his texts.

Dominico had his career to think about, his reputation, his job. He was a good cop. Yes, he bent some rules here and there, but he did more good than bad. He had a future to think about and a long life ahead of him. He wasn't about to let Brett ruin it for him, and he knew it was just a matter of time before Brett said something. *Some unknown button, some unknown trigger, and then, what?* A ruined life that didn't deserve being ruined. His life ruined.

Dominico was not about to let that happen.

If Brett would just talk to him, just listen to him, he was sure he could have worked it all out. They would have come to an agreement that would have benefitted both of them. He was sure of it.

Sitting at the kitchen table in the McGovern home, Dominico made a decision. He reasoned that it was the only option open to him. It wasn't his fault he had to make this decision. Brett forced him into it by not speaking to him.

Dominico wasn't sure how he felt about it. Maybe a little sad, perhaps frustrated, maybe even angry. But in the end, it didn't matter. Not even a little.

Dominico made a decision and it was all Brett's fault. Brett's fault, not his.

CHAPTER SIXTY-ONE

East of Round Rock, Navajo Indian Reservation, Arizona

He wore a red plaid shirt under his leather vest, well-worn jeans and scuffed leather cowboy boots. His long gray hair was tied in a braid that trailed down his back, the tip secured with a leather strap. On his gray head was a beat up and sweat-stained cowboy hat. His callused hands were dark bronze and his kind face was deeply wrinkled, resembling a saddlebag with eyes. He was taller than George, but he knew that wouldn't last for long, because George was growing.

For mid-September and what normally should have been Indian Summer, the desert was chilly on this beautiful late morning. The blue sky was clear, the air crisp, and on any other day, George's grandfather would have reveled in it.

But the sheep below him were restless, milling around the pasture without grazing and on the other side of the stand of pine. He could hear the roan stomping and snorting.

Grandfather stood up, stared at the sky and began to chant, fingering the turquoise and leather necklace that George had made for him.

The thought became crystal clear in his mind. It was beginning.

• • •

It was warm, almost stuffy in the classroom. Science was one of George's favorite subjects and Mr. Crandall was one of his favorite teachers, but George found himself staring out the window at the small staff parking lot. Only, he wasn't staring at the parking lot. He was staring out beyond it, and at the same time, within.

Rebecca, who was his lab partner, gently nudged him in the arm to get his attention and when George didn't respond to that, she jabbed him in the ribs.

"What?" he asked vaguely.

"George, are you okay?" Crandall asked. He walked over from across the room where he had been watching him and was puzzled, if not concerned. He placed a hand on his shoulder, but George didn't seem to notice.

Without looking at him, George first shook his head, but then nodded, and said, "What?"

Crandall and Rebecca looked at each other and then back at George.

By this time, the class had stopped working and all eyes were on George.

He stood up from his stool, pushed away from his lab station, and stood at the window facing east, holding onto the turquoise and leather necklace that he had made, one that was a twin to the one he had given his grandfather.

Rebecca stood up next to him to see what George was staring at, but saw nothing other than a handful of staff cars and three buses parked and waiting for the students to board them so their drivers could take them home at the end of the school day.

The other students in the class half-stood, leaned and craned their necks to stare out of the window, but no one saw anything out of the ordinary.

As he held his turquoise necklace, George whispered in his native tongue. Both Crandall and Rebecca caught only a few of the words, but not enough of them to fully understand what he was whispering.

George knew something was happening to him. What panicked him was that whatever he was experiencing had never happened to him before, yet, he wasn't actually sure what *was* happening. The only thing George knew for certain was that he needed to speak to his grandfather, and he needed to speak to him right away.

CHAPTER SIXTY-TWO

Fishers, Indiana

Brett walked home from school, but took his time so Bobby wouldn't be far behind him in case his uncle was there waiting for him. He slowed his walk and searched the street. There were a couple of cars and a blue van, but not his uncle's car, and that was a relief.

He used the code for the garage, opened the back door, took off his shoes and dropped his backpack near the hallway that led to his room. As was his ritual, he got a glass from the cupboard, went to the refrigerator, used the ice dispenser to get a couple of ice cubes, and then filled his glass with water. Then he opened the refrigerator door, found an orange and went to the sink to peel it. He stuffed the rinds into the disposal, turned it on and ran water into the sink to wash them down. He took the orange and his glass of ice water back to the kitchen table and ate it.

Bobby came into the kitchen. "Hey."

"Hey."

Bobby dropped his bag near Brett's, went to the fridge and took out the orange juice. He went to the cupboard and took out a glass, filled it up, drank about half, and refilled it to the top. Then he sat down at the table with Brett.

Brett knew Bobby was going to ask him for the millionth time about him and Uncle Tony, so he went to the dishwasher, opened it, placed his glass on the top rack, and then picked up his backpack and walked down the hall to his bedroom.

He changed his clothes to shorts, a t-shirt, and basketball shoes. He stuck his head into Bobby's room and not seeing him there, walked back to the kitchen.

Bobby hadn't moved.

"I'm going back to school to play some basketball."

Bobby nodded.

Brett studied his brother's face. "What's wrong?"

Bobby shrugged, but didn't take his eyes off the glass he held.

Brett sat down next to him. "What's wrong?" He asked again.

"I have my piano recital tonight, and I've never played in front of anyone before."

"You don't have to worry. You're really good."

His little brother looked up at him, shocked.

"What, you don't think I listen to you?"

Bobby shook his head.

Brett smiled and said, "Sometimes, when you practice, mom and I come out to the kitchen and listen to you."

"You do?"

"We know you don't like anyone listening to you, but you're really good, Bobby." Dumbfounded, Bobby didn't know what to say. "You are. That song, *Mandolin Wind*, I like that one the best."

"You listen to me singing?"

"You have a good voice. Mom likes that Kip Moore song."

"*Hey Pretty Girl?*"

"Yeah, that one."

Bobby shrugged. "It would sound better on guitar."

Brett punched him lightly on his arm. "Bobby, you're really good."

"But tonight, I'll be playing in front of mom, dad, Grandma Dominico, and a bunch of other people. And I have to play classical crap," he added with a "Blaha," and his tongue sticking out.

Brett laughed. "And you'll do great."

Bobby smiled at him and shrugged.

"You wanna go play basketball with me?"

Bobby thought about it, almost said yes, but said, "Nah, I better practice."

"You sure? We can use one more guy."

"No, I better practice."

"Okay. You're really good, Bobby. Don't worry about it. I bet you'll be the best one there."

"Thanks."

With his hand on the doorknob, Brett stopped and stared at his brother.

Bobby turned around. "What?"

Brett wanted to tell him he loved him, something that he couldn't ever remember telling him. He wanted to tell him that he was sorry he didn't do more with him, that he was sorry they never talked or hung out. He wanted to apologize for not being a very good big brother. Mostly, he wanted to tell him that he was proud of him, and that from now on, he'd do better.

"What?" Bobby asked again.

"Nothin'. I'll see you later, okay?"

"Yeah. See you later."

Brett went back into the garage, found his bike, pulled it out of the garage and shut the garage door behind him. Then he jumped on the bike and peddled out of the driveway without looking back.

He took his time, peddling slowly.

No one was on the street and there wasn't any traffic. He came to a stop sign and thought about blowing right through it like he had done hundreds and thousands of times, and not knowing why, he slowed to a stop.

A blue van pulled up next to him and the sliding door opened. Brett felt rough, strong hands pull him off the bike and clamp a damp smelly cloth over his mouth and nose. His bike fell to the pavement. He tried to fight back, but the cloth... the smell....

The sliding door closed and the van pulled away from the stop sign. Brett tried to scream for help. He tried to fight back. He tried to push the hands away, but they were too strong. He tried to hold his breath, but it was too late. He felt himself getting drowsy, sleepy, and then there was darkness. Nothing.

Brett was gone.

A half a block behind, Tony Dominico watched the brief struggle. He watched them pull Brett off the bike and into the van and watched the van pull away and drive down the street.

Dominico tried to summon up a feeling, any feeling, but nothing came to him. Nothing at all. It was all Brett's fault anyway, Brett's fault. Not his.

SNEEK PEEK

STOLEN LIVES

Where do the children go between the black night and the darkest day?
Where do the children go and who's that deadly piper who leads them away?
—Hooters, 1985

Tuck you in, warm within, keep you free from sin, til the Sandman he comes.
Sleep with one eye open, gripping your pillow tight . . .
We're off to never, never land . . .
—Metallica, 1990

CHAPTER ONE

The boy's muscles ached and he longed to stretch out, but the handcuffs prevented him from doing so. His head hit the steel wall of the dirty van each time Frank drove over a rock, or a rut, or pothole in the dirt road. The boy's neck and shoulders had grown stiff from trying to cushion the blows. He shifted sideways so his arms could take more of the pounding, but that was even more uncomfortable. He leaned as tightly against the wall as he could, pushing with his heels, but slipped on a McDonald's bag, frowning at the mustard and pickle juice on his pants' leg.

The man wearing the baseball cap pulled low to his sunglasses merely glanced at the boy, but gave no hint of emotion. The boy had never seen him before, that is, at least he didn't think he did. The way the man looked at him, showing no emotion, no expression bothered him, but he wasn't going to give into that, so he ended up ignoring him, just like the man wearing the baseball cap seemed to ignore the boy and the other two men in the van.

Ron, however, who sat in the passenger seat, turned around and glared at him, his thick lips pulled back in a sneer. The boy looked away and stared at the tips of his worn-out shoes. His big toe poked out of one and the sole flapped on the other. When the boy guessed that the big man wasn't watching him any longer, and when he felt the man wearing the baseball cap wasn't watching, he turned back cautiously and strained to see out the windshield. Red fingers of rock poked the blue horizon. Bulky buttes formed walls on either side of the van, like impatient onlookers at a passing funeral procession.

The boy guessed they were still in Arizona. The last road sign he saw mentioned Tuba City, but that was before they left asphalt and turned onto the dirt road.

"How much farther?" Ron asked the driver impatiently.

Frank turned onto a gravel road, crossed a cattle gate, and slowed to a stop as the boy watched a cloud of dust envelop the front of the van. Frank stared intently out the windows in all directions. Satisfied, he nodded and said, "'Bout a good a place as any."

The two men in the front got out of the van and the boy braced himself. He had suspected, maybe deep down knew what was going to happen. For the better part of a year, the boy had taken trips in the back of a van, sometimes handcuffed, sometimes drugged, as he was driven from one city to the next.

The man wearing the baseball cap and sunglasses sat in the van, staring at the boy, still showing no emotion and not interacting with either of the two men or with the boy. The boy looked at him, expecting him to say or do something, but he didn't. He merely sat staring at him. Or at least, the boy thought he might be staring at him. With the sunglasses, he couldn't tell if his eyes were open or closed.

The side door slid open and Ron yanked the boy's legs toward him. The boy tried to slow himself down, but the man was too strong. Before he knew it, both shoes were off and flung into the van. His socks followed shortly after that. Then Ron ripped off the boy's shirt and threw that into the van as well.

His eyes wild, the boy tried to kick, but the man was too big, too strong, and moved too quickly. With the boy's hands cuffed behind his back, he was defenseless. The man slapped the boy in the face, and then slapped him again.

"Not in the van!" Frank barked. "Just get his clothes off and bring him out here. We don't want a mess to clean up."

The man opened the boy's jeans and pulled them off along with his underwear, tossing them in the pile with the shoes, socks and what was left of the boy's shirt. Then, he grabbed an ankle and yanked him out of the van with a thud. The boy hit his head on the door frame, but he didn't yell. No. He wouldn't give them the satisfaction.

"Get up!" The fat man said to him.

When the boy didn't move fast enough, the fat man kicked him.

The boy stumbled awkwardly to his feet and faced both men. Never more than then, facing those two men, knowing what was about to happen, did he miss his mother. He had never forgotten her face. How her green eyes danced when she smiled, how her nose turned up at the end—a ski slope he had teased her about. He remembered her gentle touch, her soothing voice, and the perfume she wore when she went out with dad. Never more in the whole year he was gone did he miss her more than in that instant.

"Start walkin'," Frank said, exhaling smoke and tossing the last of a cigarette to the sand.

The boy walked slowly, the hot desert sand burning the soles of his feet. Now and then, Ron would give him a shove and the boy would stumble, but not fall down.

The man wearing the baseball cap got out of the van, but stood close to it. He didn't like the openness of the desert. He didn't like the sheep grazing up on the side of the hill. He tried to look that direction, but even with his sunglasses, he was staring into the sun and had to turn away. There was something about the place that gave the man an unsettled feeling. There was something he didn't like that was more than just the vast expanse of desert, so he stayed by himself and leaned against the side of the van near the passenger door and watched the two men and the boy.

"It's too fuckin' hot for this shit," the fat man grumbled quietly so the man wearing the baseball cap didn't hear him. "We deserve more money."

Frank said nothing, but wiped sweat off his face with the back of his hand and then felt for the gun in his belt.

"Okay, that's far enough," he said.

The boy turned around and faced both men. "You're going to kill me." It was a statement, not a question, as if facing them and seeing the gun made it all more real. Final.

"Yeah."

"Just fuckin' do him and let's go," Ron said.

Frank shrugged at the boy as if to say, *What am I supposed to do?*

A tear ran down the boy's face as he sobbed, "I wanna go home!"

"Yeah, sure," Ron said with a laugh.

"Why?"

Frank shrugged, waved the gun and said, "We don't need you anymore."

The boy looked down at the ground and then up at the men.

"I want to go home," the boy said again.

"Sorry, kid," Frank said, popping the cartridge and then palming it back into ready position, "Got orders."

"No one will find me," the boy said in panic.

Ron laughed and then spit. "That's the fuckin' point!"

The thought of being left alone in this place, this desert, with no one or nothing around him except for some sheep grazing in the distance and a hawk circling high up in the sky, made him feel desperate.

"Please?"

"Sorry kid," Frank said, walking behind him, putting a hand to the boy's shoulder, making him kneel down. "You won't feel a thing."

The boy shut his eyes, steeling himself against the blast of the gun.

Frank stepped behind and away from the boy, aimed at the back of the boy's head and pulled the trigger twice. The boy fell forward, still handcuffed, his face in the hot desert sand.

Frank was right. The boy never felt a thing.

CHAPTER TWO

George Tokay sat among the pinion pine and Joshua trees on the side of the mountain after he had hidden his horse behind the ridge. He heard the van even before it had appeared in the distance and had watched as it drove onto his grandfather's land, suspecting rustlers. Because the land where his family's sheep grazed was so remote, it happened often. Like his grandfather had taught him, George sat in shadow, the sun to his back. That way, anyone looking for him would be looking almost directly into the sun.

Shadow.

Hiding in the shadow fit, because Shadow was the name given to him during his coming of age ceremony, two years ago when he was twelve up on the mesa where he and his grandfather honored Father Sun. This was a ritual they had done together every day as long as he could remember, rain or shine. It began in the dark of early morning and ended as the sun peaked over the rim of the mountains. He wasn't singing now, though, and he wasn't with his grandfather. He was as alone as the boy.

George felt pity for him, disgust for the men, and curiosity as to why anyone would want to strip a boy naked, handcuff him and execute him. He chewed on his lower lip and then stopped himself. His grandfather had often, too often, reminded him that one of the *Dine'*—one of the Navajo people—didn't give away one's thoughts with expressions on one's face. Eyes shut, he held his breath, then let it out slowly and evenly, calming himself. Then he raised his binoculars, studying the scene again.

The fat man with his back turned away from George and near the dead boy's feet, pissed a puddle that was quickly swallowed up by the hot sand. George watched as the fat man shook himself, then zipped up and faced the dead boy, muttering something to the tall, skinny man with the beard.

George studied the fat man's face. Thick lips, broad, flat nose, dark brown hair, slicked with something other than sweat, parted sloppily on the right side of his head. Big hands with thick, fat fingers, but too far away to tell the color of the fat man's eyes. For sure, a *biligaana*, not interested in *hozro*.

George shifted over to the tall, skinny man with the scraggly black beard, bare in spots, thick in others. Not neat, but sloppy. Something about the beard—*hiding something?* Brown hair, small hands with narrow fingers. George watched as the skinny man pulled out another cigarette—Marlboro—and smoked, looking up into the hills, almost directly at George. With the cigarette clamped in his teeth, the skinny man pulled out his pecker and he too, pissed near the dead boy's body.

George decided that, like the fat man, he was a *biligaana*, maybe Hispanic. Neither of them knew or worried about the dead boy's *chindi*, his spirit. They were both ignorant of the Way, of *hozro*, and his grandfather would be disgusted with them.

He flashed his binoculars back to the van and saw a third man, but because of the sunglasses and baseball cap, he couldn't get a good look at him. In fact, George couldn't tell if the man was particularly tall or short, slightly built or muscular, though his arms looked lean and tight. The hair under the baseball cap seemed long and dark, pulled back by the cap. George shook his head slightly in frustration, and then trained his binoculars back on the two men.

He watched both men discuss something while standing on either side of the dead boy, the fat man doing most of the listening. George shook his head, angry at how they defiled the boy, first pissing at the boy's feet, then talking over him like they would over a kitchen table.

Finally, he watched them walk back, where all three men got into the van.

George studied the van. Chevy—newer looking. Black or navy blue, probably stolen. His cousin, Leonard, worked out of the Navajo Nation Police station at Window Rock and stolen cars with stolen plates were big crimes on the rez. So were murder, rape, rustling and everything else that went on in the world. His grandfather lectured him that the *Dine'* were losing their way and becoming more like the *biligaana*.

George didn't move from his spot until the van had driven from sight, and just to be safe, George waited another twenty minutes before standing and stowing his binoculars in one of the saddlebags. He took out his canteen and drank warm water, wiping some across his face. Then he mounted Nochero, the big black stallion he befriended two years previous, faced it down the hill and fingered the turquoise arrowhead around his neck.

A talisman to ward off evil.

And angry *chindi*.

Just to be safe, in case the talisman didn't work, he pulled the .22 from the scabbard.

George stopped about twenty-five yards away, what he thought was a safe distance. Nochero, impatient to get moving again, stomped its front hoof into the sand, flicked its tail at flies, snorting softly. George patted the stallion's neck and then dismounted.

He pulled off his boots and pulled out a pair of moccasins from his saddlebags. He sat down, pulled his socks off and shook sand from them before stuffing them into his boots. Then, after slipping into his moccasins, George stood up and faced the dead boy.

The Navajo boy of fourteen, who stood facing the death scene, was afraid of the dead boy's *chindi*. But George reasoned that if he were to help find the dead boy's killers and bring them to justice, the *chindi* would be satisfied and leave his family's land. The worldly boy of fourteen, who wanted to join the Navajo Nation police like his cousin, was simply curious. He saw this as an opportunity to win respect and admiration from his family, and his grandfather, in particular.

However, George was Navajo first and foremost. So, in a loud, calm voice, as confidently and as friendly as he could manage, said, "I have come to help find your killers. I want to help you. What was done to you wasn't right. I can only help if you allow me to come near. I bring you no harm," he bent down and as he walked toward the boy, picked up dried sticks and several stones no bigger than his fist.

"I'm coming now."

Taking care not to contaminate the crime scene, he stepped lightly, laying down the sticks and stones two yards away from the body, well away from where the two men had stood. He took the shirt off his back and tore it into narrow strips and stuffed all but one into his pockets. Then he picked up one stick and tied the strip of cloth in a knot like a kite tail and stuck the stick into the ground where the skinny man had stood, marking a footprint. He took another strip of cloth and stick, found the shell casings and marked them. Carefully, he moved to the other side of the boy, took another stick and strip of cloth and marked the fat man's footprint.

Then George knelt down and studied the body. A fly danced on the boy's shoulder, then onto the wound on his head. George waved his hand, scaring the fly away, knowing that eventually, there would be nothing he could do. He touched the boy's shoulder gently, as if in apology, then got up and finished marking footprints, the skinny man's cigarette butts, and finally, the van's tire tracks.

As he went to mark the footprints made by the man wearing the baseball cap, something caught his eye and he squatted down to study it closer. Between two tire prints, on the side of the van away from where George had sat watching the scene, he saw a dark spot on the sand. Careful not to touch or disturb it, he took one last stick and strip of cloth and marked it, thinking that it looked like blood. He knew that if it was, there might be more in or on the van. At some point, the men must have hurt the boy before killing him.

At last, after marking every footprint and anything else of note, George knelt down at the boy's body and touched the boy's shoulder again.

"I will leave now, but I will be back with help. I will take care of you."

George walked away slowly, reverently, got on Nochero, took one last look at the dead boy and rode off to call his cousin.

About the Author

After having been in education for forty-four years as a teacher, coach, counselor and administrator, Joseph Lewis has retired. He is the author of seven novels, using his psychology and counseling background in crafting psychological thrillers and mysteries. He has taken creative writing and screen writing courses at UCLA and USC.

Born and raised in Wisconsin, Lewis has been happily married to his wife, Kim. Together they have three wonderful children: Wil (deceased July 2014), Hannah, and Emily. He and his wife now reside in Virginia.

Note from the Author

Human Trafficking is a blot on our society. To take anyone and force them to do things against their will is a terrible crime. However, it is my belief that to force a child to engage in sexual activity is unconscionable. This should not, must not, happen. Ever.

In 1990, I came across a story of a boy, Jacob Wetterling from St. Joseph, Minnesota, who at age eleven was abducted at gunpoint by a stranger wearing a mask in front of his little brother and his best friend. To this day, I have no idea why the tragedy of this story affected and stayed with me. It got to the point where I reached out to his parents, Jerry and Patty Wetterling, and offered my help. Honestly, I was only a high school counselor and didn't know what I could do, but I felt compelled to do something, anything.

I began to research the topic of child abduction, child sexual abuse, child safety, prevention, and education. I began speaking to parent groups, student groups, teachers, and faculty about the topic and how we can keep kids safe. It wasn't much, certainly not nearly enough, but I did what I could.

Jacob's story was the genesis of *Taking Lives*, which is the prequel of my trilogy, *Stolen Lives*, *Shattered Lives*, and *Splintered Lives*. These are works of fiction, yet based upon years of research, as well as the stories that kids and parents shared with me over the years. But it is a work of fiction, first and foremost. The statistics quoted in the stories are true, taken from the National Center for Missing and Sexually Exploited Children and FBI websites. These dedicated individuals do such great work and go unnoticed by the general public. God Bless You! And while kids are abducted, some for a long time, kids do make it back home. We've read news reports about kids who do and we rejoice. Sadly, some kids don't make it back home. Some kids are found dead.

Taking Lives and the trilogy that follows is truly meant to be a story of hope, a story of survival. It pays homage to law enforcement and other caring individuals who work to bring kids home safely.

When anyone begins naming folks to thank, one risks forgetting someone. So, I apologize ahead of time. I know I have to thank Jamie Graff, Earl Coffey, and Jim Ammons for their expertise in police, FBI, and SWAT procedure; James Dahlke for sharing his forensic science work with me; Jay Cooke, Dave Mirra and Bill Osborne for their IT expertise; and Sharon King for patience with all my medical questions. I also want to thank the folks at Sage and Sweetgrass, Robert Johnson, and various personnel at the Navajo Museum for taking the time to answer my questions about Navajo culture, tradition and language.

I want to thank Theresa Storke for her patience and her encouragement on each of the books. I want to thank Stacey Donaghy of Donaghy Literary Group for guiding my writing career at the very beginning; Natissha Hayden and the folks at True Visions Publications for giving me my first opportunity to see my books in print; and I want to thank Reagan Rothe and Black Rose Writing for their belief in me and for encouraging my writing.

Lastly, I can't tell you how supportive and encouraging my family has been. My wife, Kim, and my kids Wil (deceased July 2014), Hannah, and Emily have been so understanding and encouraging, never letting me give up and pack it in after each rejection. They stood by my side and supported me and whatever great or little success I might have as a writer, I am truly blessed for having been a husband to Kim and dad to my kids. I love you guys.

To you, the reader, thanks for taking a chance on an unknown writer, a guy who loves putting words on paper and seeing what might be made from them. I hope you continue the journey with me through the trilogy and beyond, and I hope I never disappoint you.

Word-of-mouth is crucial for any author to succeed. If you enjoyed *Taking Lives*, please leave a rating and a review online—anywhere you are able. Even if it's just a sentence or two. It would make all the difference and would be very much appreciated.

    Happy and Thoughtful Reading!
    Joe

Thank you so much for reading one of Joseph Lewis's novels.
If you enjoyed the experience, please check out our recommended
title for your next great read!

Caught in a Web by Joseph Lewis

"This important, nail-biting crime thriller about MS-13 sets the
bar very high. One of the year's best thrillers."
-*BEST THRILLERS*

View other Black Rose Writing titles at
www.blackrosewriting.com/books and use promo code
PRINT to receive a **20% discount** when purchasing.

BLACK ROSE
writing

CPSIA information can be obtained
at www.ICGtesting.com
Printed in the USA
BVHW031024040522
636050BV00003B/149